Ten Fairy Tales in Latin

Ten Fairy Tales in Latin

PAULA CAMARDELLA TWOMEY
with **SUZANNE NUSSBAUM**

Bolchazy-Carducci Publishers, Inc.
Mundelein, Illinois USA

This publication was made possible by PEGASUS, LIMITED.

Editor: Laurel Draper
Cover Design & Layout: Adam Phillip Velez
Cover Illustration: "Rotkäppchen" *Little Red Riding Hood* (1908), by Julius von Klever (1850–1924). Public Domain.

Ten Fairy Tales in Latin

Paula Camardella Twomey
with Suzanne Nussbaum

© 2013 Bolchazy-Carducci Publishers, Inc.
All rights reserved.

Bolchazy-Carducci Publishers, Inc.
1570 Baskin Road
Mundelein, Illinois 60060
www.bolchazy.com

Printed in the United States of America
2013
by United Graphics

ISBN 978-0-86516-791-9

Contents

	How to Use This Book in Your Classroom	vii
1.	*Auricoma et Ursī Trēs*	1
2.	*Palliolātella*	7
3.	*Cinerellula*	13
4.	*Gallīna Rūfa*	19
5.	*Homunculus Condītus*	23
6.	*Trēs Hircī Asperī*	29
7.	*Trēs Porcellī*	35
8.	*Nivea et Septem Nānī*	41
9.	*Fistulātor Versicolor Hamelīnus*	49
10.	*Puella Pulchra Quae Dormiēbat*	55
	Grammar Notes	61
	Grammar Exercises	79
	Latin to English Glossary	111

How to Use This Book in Your Classroom

As a Class Reader

- Choose a fairy tale to read with your class.
- Review the vocabulary list with your students before reading.
- Assign parts to different class members.
- Read aloud for comprehension and new vocabulary.
- Encourage dramatic interpretation.
- Review vocabulary after reading aloud in class.
- Complete the puzzle or activity that follows each fairy tale to reinforce vocabulary.
- Refer to the Grammar Notes on page 61 as needed to review grammatical structures that occur in the fairy tale.

As a Mini-Drama

- Choose a fairy tale to read and perform.
- Read through the story with your students to decode any difficult vocabulary.
- Select the required number of student actors, and ask students to practice reading the fairy tale with a partner.
- Design a simple scenery and costumes, and collect props and costumes for the drama.

- Allow actors to read from their script, or use cue cards to allow reading from a distance.
- Direct the narrator to stand to the side of the "stage" for all narrations.
- Digitally record the mini-drama if desired.

As a Puppet Show

- Choose a fairy tale to read and perform.
- Read through the story with your students to decode any difficult vocabulary.
- Choose student actors to read from behind a stage or puppet stand, and choose puppeteers to manipulate puppets, dolls, or objects.
- Ask students to practice reading the fairy tale with a partner.
- Make sock puppets or collect stuffed animals, hand puppets, or marionettes for the puppet theater.
- Actors and puppeteers must coordinate dialogue lines with puppet actions.
- The narrator can sit in front of the set, in a rocking chair (if available), as if to simulate the telling of a children's story.
- Digitally record the puppet show if desired.

Props and Costumes

- Keep a box for props and costumes in the classroom. Collect, reuse, and interchange props for many of the fairy tales.

1. *Auricoma et Ursī Trēs*

Vocabulary

aliquis, aliquid someone, something
aureus, -a, -um golden
Auricoma, -ae, *f.* Goldilocks
calidus, -a, -um hot
commodus, -a, -um comfortable
cōnsūmō, cōnsūmere, cōnsūmpsī, cōnsūmptus to eat up
dēnārius, -ī, *m.* denarius (silver coin)
dūrus, -a, -um hard
emō, emere, ēmī, emptus to buy
frāctus, -a, -um broken
frīgidus, -a, -um cold
gustō, gustāre, gustāvī, gustātus to taste
humilis, humile simple
iānuam pulsāre to knock on the door
ientāculum, -ī, *n.* breakfast
iste, ista, istud that (of yours, that awful)
lectus, -ī, *m.* bed
mediocris, mediocre middle-sized, medium

mollis, molle soft
nātus, -a, -um + (number) + **annōs** (X) years old
patella, -ae, *f.* bowl
placeō, placēre, placuī + *dat.* to please
  placetne (vōbīs)? does it suit (you)?, is that OK?
pretium, -ī, *n.* price
  pretiō, *abl. of price* for a price
probō, probāre, probāvī, probātus to test, to try
puls, pultis, *f.* porridge
quiēs, quiētis, *f.* rest
  sē quiētī dare to rest (*lit.,* give oneself to rest)
quisque, quidque each one
recumbō, recumbere, recubuī to lie down
rēgia, -ae, *f.* (royal) palace
sella, -ae, *f.* chair
ursa, -ae, *f., and* **ursus, -ī,** *m.* bear
  ursulus, -ī, *m.* bear cub
vendō, vendere, vendidī, venditus to sell

Auricoma et Ursī Trēs

Nārrātor: Vōs laetī excipimus ad līberōrum theātrum. Hodiē vōbīs fābulam dē puellā Auricomā et Ursīs Tribus agimus. Ecce casa Ursōrum Trium: hīc habitant Ursus Pater, Ursa Māter, et parvulus īnfāns, quī est Ursulus. Ursus Pater est maximus; Ursa Māter est mediocris; Ursulus est minimus. Casa Ursōrum est humilis sed commoda: in casā sunt culīna, tablīnum, cubiculum. Secunda hōra est; māter ientāculum parat. Pultem coquit et in trēs patellās pōnit.

Ursa Māter: Puls est parāta, sed calidissima est. Necesse est nōbīs in silvā ambulāre. Cum domum redierimus, pultem edere poterimus.

Nārrātor: Ursī Trēs iam ē casā exeunt. Ecce, puella sex annōs nāta ad casam venit. Puella est pulchra; crīnēs eī aureī sunt, itaque Auricomam omnēs eam appellant. Auricoma iānuam pulsat, sed nēmō iānuam aperit; nēmō est in casā. Puella iānuam aperit; in casam intrat. Mēnsam videt. Ecce! Sunt trēs patellae pultis plēnae in mēnsā. Sunt patella maxima, patella mediocris, patella minima. Patellam quemque probat Auricoma. Prīmum dē patellā maximā gustat.

Auricoma: Illa puls est calidior! Ēheu!

Nārrātor: Deinde dē patellā mediocrī gustat.

Auricoma: Ēheu! Ista puls est frīgidior!

Nārrātor: Tandem dē patellā minimā gustat.

Auricoma: Euge! Haec puls est optima!

Nārrātor: Et omnem pultem cōnsūmpsit. Tum, pulte cōnsūmptā, Auricoma ad tablīnum it, quod sedēre vult. Sunt trēs sellae in tablīnō. Trēs sellās videt puella: sellam maximam, sellam mediocrem, sellam minimam. In quāque sellā sedet. Prīmum in sellā maximā sedet.

Auricoma: Illa sella est dūrior! Ēheu!

Nārrātor: Deinde in sellā mediocrī sedet.

Auricoma: Ēheu! Ista sella est mollior!

Nārrātor: Tandem in sellā minimā sedet.

Auricoma: Euge! Haec sella est optima!

Nārrātor: Sed sella subitō frācta est. Auricoma ad solum cadit. Nunc, sellā frāctā, puella est dēfessa et cubitum it. In cubiculum intrat: trēs lectōs videt: lectum maximum, lectum mediocrem, lectum minimum. Auricoma omnēs lectōs probat. Prīmum lectum maximum probat.

Auricoma: Quam dūrus est lectus ille! Ēheu!

Nārrātor: Deinde lectum mediocrem probat.

Auricoma: Ēheu! Quam mollis est lectus iste!

Nārrātor: Tandem lectum minimum probat.

Auricoma: Euge! Hic lectus est optimus!

Nārrātor: Statim puella in lectō minimō recumbit et sē quiētī dat.
    Brevī tempore Ursī Trēs domum redeunt. Iānuam aperiunt et in casam intrant. Ad mēnsam appropinquant. Patellās in mēnsā spectant.

Ursus Pater: Aliquis dē patellā meā ēdit.

Ursa Māter: Aliquis dē patellā meā ēdit.

Ursulus: Aliquis dē patellā meā ēdit, et omnem pultem cōnsūmpsit!

Nārrātor: Ursī Trēs ad tablīnum eunt. Sellās in tablīnō spectant.

Ursus Pater: Aliquis in sellā meā sēdit.

Ursa Māter: Aliquis in sellā meā sēdit.

Ursulus: Aliquis in sellā meā sēdit, et nunc sella frācta est!

Nārrātor: Tum Ursī Trēs in cubiculum intrant. Lectōs in cubiculō spectant.

Ursus Pater: Aliquis in lectō meō dormīvit!

Ursa Māter: Aliquis in lectō meō dormīvit!

Ursulus: Aliquis in lectō meō dormīvit—et adhūc dormit. Ecce!

Nārrātor: Clāmōrēs Ursōrum Auricomam excitant. Puella sollicita surgit.

Auricoma: Quid accidit? Ubi sum?

Ursus Pater: Ursī Trēs sumus. Es apud nōs. Vīsne amīca nostra esse? Ubi habitās tū?

Auricoma: Ita vērō, amīca esse volō. Ego quoque in silvā habitō.

Ursulus: Vīsne manēre hīc apud nōs, amīca?

Auricoma: Eugepae! Ita vērō. Grātiās vōbīs agō.

Nārrātor: Etiam nunc, Auricoma et Ursī Trēs sunt amīcissimī.

Fīnis tortus:

Auricoma: Quid accidit? Ubi sum?

Ursus Pater: Ursī Trēs sumus. Es apud nōs. Hanc casam vendere volumus—vīsne eam emere? Parvō pretiō vendimus: mille dēnāriīs modo.

Auricoma: Haec casa mihi placet. Casam amō. Eam emere volō.

Ursulus: Euge! In domū novā et maiōre habitāre volō. Et novam sellam habēre volō. Mea sella frācta est.

Auricoma: Mihi placet. Ecce! Mille dēnāriōs vōbīs trādō. Placetne vōbīs?

Nārrātor: Etiam nunc Auricoma in casā Ursōrum Trium habitat. Sed Ursī Trēs in magnā rēgiā habitant.

AURICOMA ET URSĪ TRĒS CROSSWORD PUZZLE

Complete the following puzzle using vocabulary words from **Auricoma et Ursī Trēs**. Use the nominative singular form for nouns, the masculine nominative singular for adjectives, and the present active infinitive for verbs.

Across
1. chair
4. small
6. big
8. middle-sized
10. friend
12. palace
13. porridge
14. to buy
15. hard
16. to taste

Down
2. bed
3. broken
5. hot
7. cold
9. to sell
11. (male) bear

2. Palliolātella

VOCABULARY

accidit, accidere, accidit to happen
aegrōtō, aegrōtāre, aegrōtāvī to be sick
aliēnus, -a, -um foreign, strange
amābō please (*lit.*, I will love [you])
avia, -ae, *f.* grandmother
careō, carēre, caruī to lack, be without (+ *abl.*)
cēlō, cēlāre, cēlāvī, cēlātus to hide
  sē cēlāre to hide oneself
dolābra, -ae, *f.* ax
flōs, flōris, *m.* flower
foedus, -a, -um foul, ugly
imprīmīs, *adv.* especially
incolumis, incolume unhurt
induō, induere, induī, indūtus to put on (clothing)
  indūtus, -a, -um dressed in (+ *abl.*)
latrīna, -ae, *f.* bathroom
lignātor, lignātōris, *m.* woodcutter

loquor, loquī, locūtus sum to speak
medicāmen, medicāminis, *n.* medicine
necō, necāre, necāvī, necātus to kill
palliolum, -ī, *n.* cloak
  Palliolātella, -ae, *f.* Little Red Riding Hood
pārens, pārentis (participle of **pārēre**), obedient
perīculōsus, -a, -um dangerous
propius, *compar. adv.* closer, nearer
quid, *adv.* why?
rāna, -ae, *f.* frog
ruber, rubra, rubrum red
sīc, *adv.* thus, like this, in this way
sportella, -ae, *f.* basket
tantus, -a, -um so great, so big
  tantō, *adv.* (by) so much
vādō, vādere to go, hurry, rush

Palliolātella

Nārrātor: Vōs ad līberōrum theātrum laetī excipimus. Hodiē vōbīs fābulam dē Palliolātellā agimus.

In silvā puella formōsissima septem annōs nāta habitat. Est puella pulchra et bona et prūdēns, quae imprīmīs mātrī semper pāret. Quod palliolum rubrum semper gerit, Palliolātella appellātur.

Diē quōdam, māter Palliolātellae sīc loquitur:

Māter: Heu, avia tua, Palliolātella, graviter aegrōtat. Cibō atque medicāmine caret. Ad casam aviae, amābō, ī; hanc sportellam fer, cibī atque medicāminis plēnam. Cavē tamen, fīlia mea, cavē lupum! Nōlī cum lupō loquī!

Palliolātella: Itā vērō, māter. Intellegō. Valē! Nōbīscum mox conveniēmus.

Nārrātor: Palliolātella, dum per silvam ambulat, carmen cantat, flōrēs spectat atque multōs aviae carpit.

Palliolātella: Lalla lalla. Flōrēs aviae quam pulchrōs carpō!

Nārrātor: Lupus tamen ad extrēmam silvam appāret. Puellae sīc loquitur:

Lupus: Salvē, Palliolātella. Quid tū hīc in silvā? Quō vādis, palliolō rubrō tuō indūta?

Palliolatella: Cibum atque medicāmen aviae ferō, et flōrēs eī carpere volō. Heu, graviter aegrōtat avia.

Lupus: Ō rēs miserābilis! Abīre tamen mihi necesse est. Valē, Palliolātella! Euge!

Nārrātor: Tum lupus ad aviae casam celeriter currit. Iānuam pulsat.

Avia: Quis iānuam pulsat?

Lupus: Palliolātella sum, avia.

Avia: Intrā, intrā, cāra. Ēheu! Palliolātella nōn es. Lupus es!

Lupus: Itā vērō. Lupus sum. Age, ī in latrīnam! Da mihi vestīmenta tua! Ibi in latrīnā tē cēlā!

Nārrātor: Avia perterrita in latrīnam it ut sē cēlet. Lupus, vestīmentīs aviae indūtus, in lectō eius iacet. Eō ipsō tempore aliquis iānuam pulsat.

Lupus: Quis iānuam pulsat?

Palliolātella: Palliolātella sum, avia.

Lupus: Intrā, intrā, cāra. Venī hūc, prope lectum. Quid mihi fers?

Palliolātella: Flōrēs, cibum, medicāmen tibi ferō.

Lupus: Euge! Venī hūc, venī propius, ad lectum. Volō tē ācrius vidēre.

Palliolātella: Tū tamen, avia, tibi dissimilis es. Tantae aurēs tibi sunt!

Lupus: Tantō tē ācrius audiam.

Palliolātella: Tantī oculī tibi sunt!

Lupus: Tantō tē ācrius videam.

Palliolātella: Tantī dentēs tibi sunt!

Lupus: Tantō tē celerius edam. Euge!

Palliolātella: Ēheu! Ō mē miseram!

Nārrātor: Eō ipsō tempore lupus ē lectō salit. Simul atque Palliolātellam corripere temptat, lignātor quīdam prope casam aviae ambulat.

Lignātor: Quālēs clāmōrēs audiō? Quid accidit?

Palliolātella: Ō lignātor! Quam laeta tē videō! Ecce, lupus est in casā aviae. Ubi est avia?

Lignātor: Lupus adest? Lupus in hāc casā? Age, lupe, abī nec posteā umquam redī! Sī redībis, tē dolābrā meā necābō.

Nārrātor: Lupus perterritus statim ē casā in silvam effugit, numquam reditūrus. Avia ē latrīnā exit.

Avia: Tibi grātiās, lignātor, maximās agō. Ō Palliolātella! Incolumis es?

Palliolātella: Itā vērō, avia!

Avia: Nōlī posteā cum lupō loquī! Perīculōsissimum est!

Palliolātella: Itā vērō, avia, id plānē intellegō.

Nārrātor: Posteā Palliolātella pārentior est, nec cum aliēnīs loquitur.

Fīnis tortus:

Lignātor: Lupus adest? Lupus in hāc casā? Age, lupe, abī nec posteā umquam redī! Sī redībis, tē dolābrā meā necābō.

Nārrātor: Lupus subitō effugere temptat. Cum lignātor eum petit, lupus in rānam quattuor oculīs pedibusque sex foedissimam vertitur. Avia ē latrīnā exit.

Avia: Rānam quam foedissimam!

Palliolātella Word Search

Translate the following words (all used in **Palliolātella**) from English into Latin. Then, find the Latin words in the Word Search below. Use the nominative singular form for nouns, the masculine nominative singular for adjectives, and the present active infinitive for verbs.

to be sick _____   door _____
to lack, to need _____   ax _____
to try _____   dressed, clad _____
to hide _____   safe and sound _____
to eat _____   unlike, dissimilar _____
little cloak _____   ugly _____
little basket _____   red _____
medicine _____

```
i a n u a s n a i d l o v u n
m p i c h u e b r n m z i z l
n e m a c i d e m b d n t v v
a a i r c e g r c d a u p f l
f e c n r t e t i z m l t b a
p r g a c b i s g o c v o u s
m n l r u o s f a t a p u d s
b e e r o i l u n a r d t o i
c s n a m t h u x b e q e x l
i a t i x l a o m g r s r o d
b u l o h f h r s i e u e h f
r i g t n z o k e d s d d g o
s m u l o i l l a p l e e b u
s p o r t e l l a f u o r i u
e r a t p m e t x x f f r t d
```

3. *Cinerellula*

Vocabulary

acerbus, -a, -um bitter, harsh
adfor, adfarī, adfatus sum to address, speak to
aliēnus, -a, -um foreign, strange
alimentum, -ī, *n.* food (usu. used in the plural)
aliquis, aliquid someone, something
angustus, -a, -um narrow
aptē, *adv.* appropriately, suitably
careō, carēre, caruī to lack (+ *abl.*)
cinis, cineris, *m.* ash
  Cinerellula, -ae, *f.* Cinderella
cōram, *prep. + abl.* in the presence of
cruciō, cruciāre, cruciāvī, cruciātus to torture
cucurbita, -ae, *f.* cucumber
epulae, -ārum, *f. pl.* banquet
ēvanēscō, ēvanēscere, ēvanuī to vanish
faunus, -ī, *m.* fairy, woodland sprite
flētus, -ūs, *m.* weeping
habitus, -ūs, *m.* dress (appearance)
idōneus, -a, -um suitable

intervallum, -ī, *n.* space between, gap
lacrimō, lacrimāre, lacrimāvī to cry
libet, libēre, libuit it is pleasing (+ *infin.*)
lūdibrium, -ī, *n.* laughingstock, (source of) derision
margarīta, -ae, *f.* pearl
meminī, meminisse to remember
mendacium, -ī, *n.* lie, falsehood
mōmentum, -ī, *n.* importance
monīle, monīlis, *n.* necklace
mūs, mūris, *m.* mouse
nīmīrum, *adv.* doubtless, undoubtedly
nōscō, nōscere, nōvī, nōtus to know
noverca, -ae, *f.* stepmother
nuptiae, -ārum, *f. pl.* wedding
oblīviscor, oblīviscī, oblītus sum + *gen.* to forget
opus, operis, *n.* work, task
patrōna, -ae, *f.* protectress, patroness, "godmother"

Vocabulary (Continued)

persolvō, persolvere, persolvī, persolūtus to pay (back), to render
pīlentum, -ī, *n.* lady's carriage
proficīscor, proficīscī, profectus sum to set out
rēgius, -a, -um royal
revertō, revertere, revertī to return, revert
saltō, saltāre, saltāvī to dance
sinus, -ūs, *m.* breast, bosom
solea, -ae, *f.* shoe
stola, -ae, *f.* (woman's long) dress
taenia, -ae, *f.* headband
tintinnabulum, -ī, *n.* bell
tintinnō, tintinnāre to ring
turpis, turpe shameful, base, disgraceful
vestītus, -ūs, *m.* (suit of) clothing
vitreus, -a, -um made of glass

CINERELLULA

Nārrātor: Vōs ad līberōrum theātrum laetī excipimus. Hodiē vōbīs fābulam dē Cinerellulā agimus. Est puella quae cum patre, cum novercā, cum duābus novercae fīliābus habitat. Sōla rem domesticam cūrat: vestīmenta lavat, cēnam parat, domum pūrgat. Puella dulcis est, sed acerba est noverca, novercae fīliae sunt turpēs.

Diē quōdam, noverca sīc loquitur:

Noverca: Fortūnātissimae sumus! Ad epulās regiās vocātae sumus. Fīlius rēgis uxōrem ēliget.

Fīlia Novercae Prīma: Ad epulās rēgiās ībō!

Fīlia Novercae Altera: Ad epulās rēgiās ībō!

Cinerellula: Ego quoque ad epulās rēgiās ībō.

Noverca: Ībis sī omnia opera confēceris. Multa tibi facienda sunt hodiē: vestīmenta lavanda, alimenta coquenda. Num vestītum idōneum habēs? Minimē crēdō!

Nārrātor: Cinerellula misera tōtum diem ad vesperum labōrat. Noverca et fīliae epulīs rēgiīs sē parant.

Noverca: Mihi hanc stolam, stulta, compōne!

Fīlia Novercae Prīma: Mihi crīnēs taeniīs, fatua, compōne!

Fīlia Novercae Altera: Mihi illās soleās, turpissimum, affer!

Nārrātor: Tempus est ad epulās rēgias proficīscī. Cinerellula quoque ad eās proficīscī vult.

Cinerellula: Mē, sī vultis, exspectāte! Ad epulās rēgiās īre volō.

Noverca: Parāta tamen nōn es. Neque vestītum idōneum, neque soleās novās, neque gemmās ūllās geris. Nōbīscum īre nōn potes. Valē!

Nārrātor: Ō miseram Cinerellulam! Lacrimat; sinum flētū complet. Eō ipsō tempore Patrōna Faunōrum appāret.

Patrōna Faunōrum: Nōlī tē cruciāre, Cinerellula. Ad epulās rēgiās ībis. Prīmum tamen vestītus idōneus inveniendus erit. *(paf!)* Deinde soleae novae inveniendae erunt. *(paf!)* Postrēmō erit inveniendum monīle margarītārum. *(paf!)* Ecce, splendida es habitū, et ad epulās rēgiās ībis.

Cinerellula: At quō vehiculō, Patrōna, ad epulās ībō?

Patrōna Faunōrum: Vehiculō quōdam rēgiō. Hāc cucurbitā ūtar, et hīs mūribus *(paf!)*. Ecce pīlentum tuum rēgium!

Cinerellula: Euge! Omnia sunt splendidissima, Patrōna. Ad epulās ībō!

Patrōna Faunōrum: Manē tamen, Cinerellula. Alicuius oblīta sum maximī momentī: tibi necesse erit domum redīre ante mediam noctem. Mediā ipsā nocte omnia magica ēvānescent, omnia magica in sē revertent.

Cinerellula: Ita vērō, Patrōna, meminerō. Valē! Tibi maximās grātiās agō!

Nārrātor: Omnēs puellam pulcherrimam ad epulās ingressam magnopere admīrantur.

Fīlia Novercae Prīma: Quis est illa? Illam nōvī?

Fīlia Novercae Altera: Aliēna est.

Noverca: Pulchra nōn est. Vestītus eius est turpis. Vōs multō pulchriōrēs estis ambae!

Fīlius Rēgis: Placetne tibi, domina, ut mēcum saltēs?

Cinerellula: Mihi maximē placet.

Nārrātor: Cinerellula cum rēgis fīliō tōtam noctem saltat. Omnēs eōs admīrantur. Tin, tin, tin! *(tintinnābulum duodeciēns tintinnat).*

Cinerellula: Ēheu, mihi necesse est abīre. Media est nox. Valē!

Fīlius Rēgis: Manē, amābō tē! Cūr abīs? Eho! Quid videō? Soleam vitream videō. Solea puellae pulcherrimae est. Eam crās quaeram.

Nārrātor: Cinerellula domum redit. Posterō diē fīlius rēgis cum nūntiō ad eius domum advenit.

Nūntius: Puellam pulcherrimam soleā vitreā carentem quaerimus.

Noverca: Intrāte, intrāte. Haec solea nīmīrum alterī fīliārum meārum est. Age, eam indue.

Fīlia Novercae Prīma: Nimium angusta est pedī meō.

Fīlia Novercae Altera: Quālem dolōrem! Mihi ad pedem aptē nōn convenit!

Cinerellula: Eam induam, amābō?

Noverca: Lūdibriō nōbīs nē sīs, Cinerellula! Tibi nōn est solea vitrea!

Fīlius Rēgis: *(Novercam adfātus)* Sī libet, domina, . . . *(Cinerellulam adfātus)* Ita vērō, domina, licet tibi ut eam induās.

Cinerellula: Grātiās. Ecce, domine, mihi ad pedem aptē convenit!

Noverca: Possibile nōn est!

Fīlia Novercae Prīma: Vērum nōn est!

Fīlia Novercae Altera: Est mendācium!

Fīlius Rēgis: Vērum quidem est. Deīs grātiās persolvō! Uxor mea tū eris! Vōs tamen trēs, ē regnō meō ēgrediminī neque umquam regrediminī! Nunc, cārissima, diem nūptiīs dīcāmus.

Nārrātor: Minimō temporis intervallō fīlius rēgis Cinerellulam in mātrimōnium dūcit. Vītam beātam in perpetuum agunt.

Fīnis tortus:

Fīlius Rēgis: Vērum quidem est. Deīs grātiās persolvō! Uxor mea tū eris! Vōs tamen trēs, ē regnō meō ēgrediminī neque umquam regrediminī! Nūntiābimus apertē quam scelerōsae et impiae sītis. Nōmina vestra in Rostrīs proscrīpta populus spectābit. Nunc, cārissima, diem nūptiīs dīcāmus. Nūptiās celebrābimus cōram populō.

CINERELLULA CROSSWORD PUZZLE

Translate the clues into Latin, and write them in the spaces in the puzzle. Use masculine nominative singular form for adjectives and the present active infinitive for verbs. For nouns, use the nominative case—but pay attention to the English clue to determine whether the answer should be singular or plural. Remember that some nouns in Latin exist only in the plural.

Across
3. wedding
5. shoe, slipper
8. to cry
10. at midnight
15. godmother
17. cucumber

Down
1. necklace
2. feast
4. to wait for
6. mice
7. to dance
9. marriage
11. suitable
12. stepmother
13. to wash
14. messenger
16. palace

4. *Gallīna Rūfa*

Vocabulary

adiuvō, adiuvāre, adiūvī, adiūtus to help
anas, anatis, *f.* duck
augescō, augescere, auxī to increase, grow
crescō, crescere, crēvī, crētus to increase, grow
dissentiō, dissentīre, dissēnsī to disagree
fār, fārris, *n.* grain
farīna, -ae, *f.* flour
fēlēs, fēlis, *f.* cat
furnus, -ī, *m.* oven
gallīna, -ae, *f.* hen
iēiūnus, -a, -um hungry
iūcundus, -a, -um pleasant, delightful
messis, messis, *f.* harvest
molō, molere, moluī, molitus to grind

nequeō, nequīre, nequiī, nequītus to be unable
odor, odōris, *m.* smell
oleō, olēre, oluī to smell (of)
olfaciō, olfacere, olfēcī, to smell (something)
pānis, pānis, *m.* bread
piger, pigra, pigrum lazy
rūfus, -a, -um red
Saliī, Saliōrum, *m. pl.* priests of Mars who performed ritual dances (and held banquets)
Saliāris, Saliāre relating to the Salii
seges, segetis, *f.* the crop (of grain)
serō, serere, sēvī, satus to sow
suāviter, *adv.* sweetly
sumptuōsus, -a, -um expensive, costly, extravagant
trīticum, -ī, *n.* wheat

GALLĪNA RŪFA

Nārrātor: Vōs ad līberōrum theātrum laetī excipimus. Hodiē vōbīs fābulam dē gallīnā rufā agimus. Gallīna rūfa in vīllā magnā cum porcō et fēle et anate habitat. Pigerrimī quidem sunt porcus et fēles et anas; gallīna rūfa igitur vīllam cūrat sola. Ōlim in hortō labōrat gallīna rūfa, et rogat:

Gallīna: Quis me trīticum serere adiuvābit?

Porcus: Tē adiuvāre nōn possum.

Fēlēs: Tē adiuvāre nequeō.

Anas: Ego quoque nōn valeō.

Gallīna: Bene! Itaque id faciam ego ipsa sōla!

Nārrātor: Ergō, trīticō satō, seges augescit et crescit; gallīna rūfa inquit...

Gallīna: Quis mē messem facere adiuvābit?

Porcus: Tē adiuvāre nōn possum.

Fēlēs: Tē adiuvāre nequeō.

Anas: Ego quoque nōn valeō.

Gallīna: Bene! Itaque id faciam ego ipsa sōla!

Nārrātor: Nunc, messe factō, necesse est gallīnae rūfae farīnam facere:

Gallīna: Quis mē fār molere adiuvābit?

Porcus: Nōn possum.

Fēlēs: Nequeō.

Anas: Nōn valeō.

Gallīna: Bene! Id faciam ego ipsa sōla.

Nārrātor: Deinde, farre molitō, necesse est gallīnae rūfae pānem facere:

Gallīna: Quis me pānem facere adiuvābit?

Porcus: Nōn possum.

Fēlēs: Nequeō.

Anas: Nōn valeō.

Gallīna: Bene! Id faciam ego ipsa sōla.

Nārrātor: Tandem pānem facit gallīna rūfa, et in furnō pānem coquit.

Porcus, Fēlēs, Anas: Iūcundum odōrem olfaciō. Suāviter olet!

Gallīna: Quis mē ad pānem suāvissimum edendum adiuvābit?

Porcus: Pānem edere possum!

Fēlēs: Pānem edere queō!

Anas: Pānem edere valeō!

Gallīna: Ego tamen dissentiō. Sōla ego omnia cūrō, sōla ego omnem pānem cōnsūmō.

Nārrātor: Itaque gallīna rūfa omnem pānem cōnsūmit. Iēiunī sunt porcus et fēlēs et anas.

Fīnis tortus:

Gallīna: Ego tamen dissentiō. Sōla ego omnia cūrō, sōla ego omnem pānem cōnsūmō. Posteā apud Saliōs sum cēnātūra: epulae Saliārēs optimae sunt!

Nārrātor: Gallīna rūfa vērō ad Saliōs ad epulās sumptuōsās edendās it. Iēiūnī tamen sunt porcus et fēlēs et anas.

GALLĪNA RŪFA WORD SEARCH

Translate the following from English into Latin; then find the Latin words in the Word Search, below. Use masculine nominative singular form for adjectives and the present active infinitive for verbs. For nouns, use the nominative case—but pay attention to the English clue to determine whether the answer should be singular or plural. Remember that some nouns in Latin exist only in the plural.

hen _____
duck _____
wheat _____
crop _____
flour _____
bread _____
banquet, feast _____
to sow _____
to grind, mill _____

to eat up _____
to dine _____
to disagree _____
hungry _____
sweet _____
sweetly _____
lazy _____
pleasant _____

```
s u a v i s c g l r r v g v m
s i n a p q e n l i e o s f n
n b r a t o n e t q t x d f r
e r e r e s a q o u i a h b e
u b m l e l r e g h v r a s q
f r g l c r e o n v a a n o z
e r i t n e s s i d u f i i m
s l g i m t x x a u s t l e r
m u e r e m u s n o c r l i e
x f d h i u t c r s z i a u g
e c m n f b m u a d s t g n i
z q l i u g r n a e o i o u p
q c f f h c a b g i n c t s e
e a l u p e u e t x b u v c x
e r e l o m s i u s e m o f d
```

5. *Homunculus Condītus*

Vocabulary

afferō, afferre, attulī, allātus to bring (toward), bring along
agō, agere, ēgī, āctus + vītam to live a life *(described by an adjective)*
    beātam vītam agere to live happily ever after
altus, -a, -um deep
anus, -ūs, *f.* old woman
beātus, -a, -um blessed, happy
caput, capitis, *n.* head
cauda, -ae, *f.* tail
condītus, -a, -um spicy
crustulum, -ī, *n.* cookie
currō, currere, cucurrī to run
dēceptus, -a, -um deceived
homunculus, -ī, *m.* little man
iaceō, iacēre, iacuī to lie
iniciō, inicere, iniēcī, iniectus to throw (something) upon
laqueus, -ī, *m.* lasso
madidus, -a, -um wet
nisi, *conj.* unless
perpetuus, -a, -um eternal
    in perpetuum forever, eternally

praetereō, praeterīre, praeteriī, praeteritus to pass by
rē vērā, *adv.* in truth, for real
rīpa, -ae, *f.* bank *(of a river)*
rīsus, -ūs, *m.* laugh
rīvus, -ī, *m.* stream
rostrum, -ī, *n.* muzzle
saliō, salīre, saliī to jump
salūs, salūtis, *f.* safety
salvus, -a, -um safe
senex, senis, *m.* old man
sistō, sistere, stitī, status to stop
tam, *adv.* so
tergum, -ī, *n.* back
trānseō, trānsīre, trānsiī to go across
trānsferō, trānsferre, trānstulī, trānslātus to carry across
ulterior, ulterius, *compar. adj.* farther
vacca, -ae, *f.* cow
vulpēs, vulpis, *f.* fox

Homunculus Condītus

Nārrātor: Vōs laetī ad līberōrum theātrum excipimus. Hodiē vōbīs fābulam dē homunculō condītō agimus. Sunt anus parva, parvusque senex quī in casā habitant. Diē quōdam, anus crustulum condītum familiae coquere cōnstituit. Huic crustulō est forma hominis parvī.

Anus: Euge, suāviter olet. Hic homunculus est iam edendus.

Nārrātor: Simul atque anus homunculum ē furnō trahit, salit ille et clāmat,

Homunculus: Age! Curre, curre quam celerrimē potes! Mē edere nōn potes! Homunculus condītus sum!

Anus: Siste! Nōlī tam celeriter currere! Tē edam!

Nārrātor: Anus tamen celeriter currere nōn potest, homunculus igitur effugit.
Tum praeterit senem, quī in hortō labōrat.

Homunculus: Age! Curre, curre quam celerrimē potes! Mē edere nōn potes! Homunculus condītus sum! Ex anū effūgī; ē tē effugere poterō!

Senex: Siste! Nōlī tam celeriter currere! Tē edam!

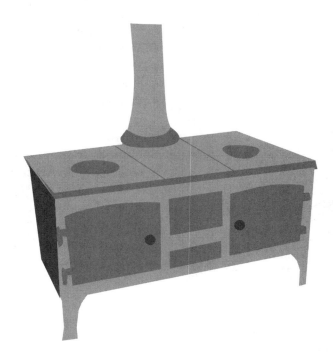

Nārrātor: Senex tamen celeriter currere nōn potest, homuculus igitur effugit.
   Tum praeterit rūsticōs quī in agrīs labōrant.

Homunculus: Agite! Currite, currite quam celerrimē potestis! Mē edere nōn potestis! Homunculus condītus sum! Ex anū effūgī; ē sene quoque; etiam ē vōbīs effugere poterō!

Rūsticī: Siste! Nōlī tam celeriter currere! Tē edēmus!

Nārrātor: Rūsticī tamen ita currere nōn possunt, homunculus igitur effugit.
   Tum praeterit vaccam quae prope viam stat.

Homunculus: Age! Curre, curre quam celerrimē potes! Mē edere nōn potes! Ex anū, ē sene, ē rūsticīs quoque effūgī. Ex tē effugere poterō!

Vacca: Siste! Nōlī ita currere! Tē edam!

Nārrātor: Vacca tamen ita currere nōn potest, homunculus igitur ex eā effugit.
   Tum praeterit vulpem quae prope rīvum iacet.

Homunculus: Age! Curre, curre quam celerrimē potes! Mē edere nōn potes! Ex anū, ē sene, ē rūsticīs, ē vaccā quoque effūgī. Ex tē effugere poterō!

Vulpēs: Euge, homuncule! Rīvus tibi trānseundus est, sī omnēs hōs effugere vīs. In caudam meam salī, et tē ad ulteriōrem rīpam trānsferam.

Homunculus: Grātiās tibi, lupe, agō. Tēcum rīvum trānsībō.

Nārrātor: Homunculus in caudam vulpis salit, et ibi sedet.

Vulpēs: Ēheu, homuncule, rīvus est altior. In tergum meum salī, nisi madidus fīās.

Homunculus: Ita vērō, vulpēs.

Nārrātor: Homunculus in tergum vulpis salit, et ibi sedet.

Vulpēs: Ēheu, homuncule, rīvus est altissimus. In caput meum salī, nisi madidus fīās.

Homunculus: Ita vērō, vulpēs.

Nārrātor: Homunculus in caput vulpis salit, et ibi sedet.

Vulpēs: Ēheu, homuncule, rīvus est quam altissimus. In rostrum meum salī, nisi madidus fīās.

Homunculus: Ita vērō, vulpēs.

Nārrātor: Homunculus in rostrum vulpis salit, et ibi sedet.

Vulpēs: Euge! Iam effugere, homuncule, nōn potes. Tē rē vērā edam.

Nārrātor: Hoc est quod accidit. Vulpēs homunculum ēdit, et vītam beātam in perpetuum ēgit.

Fīnis tortus:

Nārrātor: Eō ipsō tempore tamen homunculus laqueum quem sēcum attulit in arborēs inicit, et sē ā vulpis rostrō ad salūtem trahit. Homunculus, quī iam in arboribus salvus sedet, vulpem dēceptam magnō rīsū dērīdet.

Homunculus condītus Word Play

This activity can be done competitively, in pairs or in teams.

1. Given a sentence from the play, change the form of the character's name, as necessary, to make a new statement:

    Homunculus condītus sum!   I am the Gingerbread Man!

    I'll eat <u>the Gingerbread Man</u>!
    _____ edam!

    They will bring help to <u>the Gingerbread Man</u>!
    _____ auxilium ferent!

    <u>I am the Gingerbread Man's</u> owner / mistress!
    _____ domina sum!

    I'll tell you the story about <u>the Gingerbread Man</u>!
    Dē _____ tibi fābulam nārrābō!

2. In the story, the Gingerbread Man jumps **onto** (*in* + *acc.*) various body parts of the fox; in this exercise, change the Latin to show that he now sits **on** (*in* + *abl.*) the various body parts:

    <u>In caudam</u> vulpis salit.   Nunc in _____ vulpis sedet.
    cauda, -ae, *f.*

    <u>In tergum</u> vulpis salit.   Nunc in _____ vulpis sedet.
    tergum, -ī, *n.*

    <u>In caput</u> vulpis salit.   Nunc in _____ vulpis sedet.
    caput, capitis, *n.*

    <u>In rostrum</u> vulpis salit.   Nunc in _____ vulpis sedet.
    rostrum, -ī, *n.*

We can suppose that the Gingerbread Man, once eaten, is in the fox's innards:

He is now found in the fox's belly:

In _____ vulpis invenītur.
    venter, ventris, *m.*

6. *Trēs Hircī Asperī*

Vocabulary

ascendō, ascendere, ascendī to climb
asper, aspera, asperum rough, gruff
cadō, cadere, cecidī to fall
confestim, *adv.* immediately
corripiō, corripere, corripuī, correptus to seize
dēpellō, dēpellere, dēpulī, dēpulsus to remove
faunus, -ī, *m.* gnome, troll
herba, -ae, *f.* grass
hircus, -ī, *m.* billy goat
maior, maius (*compar.* of **magnus**) bigger
maximus, -a, -um (*superl.* of **magnus**) biggest
minimus, -a, -um (*superl.* of **parvus**) smallest

mollis, molle soft
multō (by) much
piscātor, piscātōris, *m.* fisherman
piscis, piscis, *m.* fish
pons, pontis, *m.* bridge
simul atque, *conj.* as soon as
strepitus, -ūs, *m.* racket, noise
trānseō, trānsīre, trānsiī to go across
trux, trucis fierce
tuxtax, (onomatopoeia; a thumping sound, used of falling blows on a person, in Plautus)
viridis, viride green
vir optime (*voc.*) sir
vorō, vorāre, vorāvī, vorātus to swallow up

Trēs Hircī Asperī

Nārrātor: Vōs laetī ad theātrum līberōrum excipimus. Hodiē vōbīs fābulam dē tribus hircīs asperīs agimus. Trēs hircī rūrī habitant. Cotīdiē trāns rīvum trānseunt ut herbam viridem et mollem edant. Hircīs tamen necesse est trāns pontem trānsīre sub quō habitat faunus trux. Magnum strepitum faciunt hircī trāns pontem trānseuntēs.

tuxtax tuxtax

Faunus: Quis tantum strepitum facit pontem meum trānsiēns?

Hircus Prīmus: Ego strepitum faciō, vir optime, hircus minimus.

Faunus: Eō sum ascēnsūrus ut tē cōnfestim vorem.

Hircus Prīmus: Nōlī mē vorāre, vir optime. Frāter mē sequitur multō mē maior.

Faunus: Bene, bene. Eum exspectābō.

tuxtax tuxtax

Nārrātor: Magnum strepitum faciunt hircī trāns pontem trānseuntēs.

Faunus: Quis tantum strepitum facit pontem meum trānsiēns?

Hircus Alter: Ego strepitum faciō, vir optime, hircus maior.

Faunus: Eō sum ascēnsūrus ut tē cōnfestim vorem.

Hircus Alter: Nōlī mē vorāre, vir optime. Frāter mē sequitur multō mē maior.

Faunus: Bene, bene. Eum exspectābō.

tuxtax tuxtax!

Nārrātor: Magnum strepitum faciunt hircī trāns pontem trānseuntēs.

Faunus: Quis tantum strepitum facit pontem meum trānsiēns?

Hircus Tertius: Ego strepitum faciō, vir optime, hircus maximus.

Faunus: Eō ascensūrus sum ut tē confestim vorem!

Nārrātor: Faunus trux pontem ascendit, sed, simul atque hircum maximum corripere temptat, ille faunum in rīvum inicit.

Hircus Tertius: Hircus Maximus sum, Faune trux. Neque mē neque frātrēs meōs vorāre potes.

Faunus: Ēheu! ēheu! In rīvum cecidī!

Nārrātor: Trēs Hircī asperī trāns pontem cotīdiē trānseunt. Herbam viridem et mollem edunt, nam Faunus trux ēvānuit!

Fīnis tortus:

Nārrātor: Simul atque in rīvum cecidit, Faunus trux in piscem ingentem sē vertit. Piscātōrēs quīdam illum capiunt et cōnsūmunt. Trēs hircī asperī trāns rīvum cotīdiē trānseunt et herbam viridem et mollem edunt. Trāns pontem semper trānseunt.

TRĒS HIRCĪ ASPERĪ WORD PLAY

Getting along with the fierce gnome that lives under the bridge

What are the Billy Goats Gruff (and other neighbors) doing to the fierce gnome? Match each statement with the appropriate form of the phrase <u>Faunus trux</u>:

a. Faunus trux   *nom.*   d. Faunum trucem   *acc.*
b. Faunī trucis   *gen.*   e. Faunō trucī   *abl.*
c. Faunō trucī   *dat.*   f. Faune trux   *voc.*

1. *The biggest goat will be the death of the **fierce gnome**!*
   Hircus maximus _____ exitiō erit!

2. *It's necessary for the Billy Goats Gruff to cross the **fierce gnome's** bridge.*
   Necesse est Tribus Hircīs Asperīs pontem _____ trānsīre.

3. *Watch out, **fierce gnome**; the biggest brother will be coming soon!*
   Cavē, _____; frāter maximus mox ventūrus est!

4. *If you should annoy the **fierce gnome**, little brother, tell him that your big brother will come soon!*
   Sī _____, frātercule, vexēs, dīc eī frātrem maiōrem mox ventūrum esse!

5. *The **fierce gnome** was watching as the fox devoured the Gingerbread Man.*
   _____ spectābat, dum vulpēs Homunculum condītum vorat.

6. *Since the **fierce gnome** had been killed, the Billy Goats Gruff lived happily ever after.*
   _____ necātō, Trēs Hircī Asperī vītam beātam ēgērunt.

7. *Once upon a time, Red Riding Hood sent the **fierce gnome** flowers as a gift, but this did not make him less fierce.*

Ōlim Palliolātella _____ flōrēs mūnerī dōnāvit, hoc tamen eum minus trucem nōn reddidit.

7. *Trēs Porcellī*

VOCABULARY

aēnum, -ī, *n.* copper pot
agricola, -ae, *m.* farmer
carpō, carpere, carpsī, carptus to pick, pluck
concēdō, concēdere, concessī, concessus to grant, allow
construō, construere, construxī, constructus to build
dīruō, dīruere, dīruī, dīrutus to pull apart
discēdō, discēdere, discessī to leave
dōlus, -ī, *m.* trick
dulcis, -e sweet
ferveō, fervēre, ferbuī to be boiling
fingō, fingere, finxī, fictus to form, invent
flō, flāre, flāvī, flātus to blow
   adflāre, to blow at
   inflāre, to blow upon
focus, -ī, *m.* hearth
humilis, -e humble, lowly
imperō, imperāre, imperāvī, imperātus to order
īrātus, -a, -um angry
iter, itineris, *n.* journey, trip, route
   iter facere to travel, make a journey

later, lateris, *m.* brick
libenter, *adv.* gladly, willingly
pōmum, -ī, *n.* fruit
porcellus, -ī, *m.* piglet
prior, prius (*compar. adj.*) first, sooner
quaerō, quaerere, quaesīvī, quaesītus to look for
rāmus, -ī, *m.* branch
remōtus, -a, -um far removed
sapiō, sapere, sapīvī to be tasty, to taste good
sollemne, sollemnis, *n.* religious rite, festival
strāmentum, -ī, *n.* straw
structor, structōris, *m.* builder
suāvis, suāve sweet
tēctum, -ī, *n.* roof
usque, *adv.* continually
ūva, -ae, *f.* grape
vicissim, *adv.* in turn
victus, -ūs, *m.* living
vīnea, -ae, *f.* vineyard
volō, volāre to fly

TRĒS PORCELLĪ

Nārrātor: Vōs laetī ad līberōrum theātrum excipimus. Hodiē vōbīs fābulam dē tribus porcellīs agimus. Trēs porcellī cum mātre in casā humilī habitant. Quōdam diē māter eōs iubet discēdere ut victum quaerant. Trēs porcellī itaque iter faciunt. In itinere porcellus prīmus rūsticō cuidam loquitur:

Porcellus Prīmus: Salvē, agricola. Vīsne mihi strāmenta vendere, ut casam mihi construam?

Agricola: Libenter hoc faciō!

Nārrātor: Porcellus prīmus casam sibi strāmentīs construit. Deinde, casā strāmentīs constructā, advenit lupus.

Lupus: Porcelle, porcelle, mihi concēde ut in casam ineam.

Porcellus Prīmus: Minimē! Minimē! Numquam concēdam!

Lupus: Itaque flābō, inflābō et iterum afflābō, et casam dīruam! Euge! Quam suāvis sapiet hic porcellus!

Nārrātor: Casa dīruitur; porcellus prīmus ā lupō vorātur. Itaque porcellus alter lignātōrī cuidam imperat:

Porcellus Alter: Salvē, lignātor, vīsne mihi rāmōs vendere, ut casam mihi construam?

Lignātor: Libenter hoc faciō!

Nārrātor: Itaque porcellus alter casam sibi rāmīs construit. Deinde, casā rāmīs constructā, advenit lupus.

Lupus: Porcelle, porcelle, mihi concēde ut in casam ineam.

Porcellus Alter: Minimē! Minimē! Numquam concēdam!

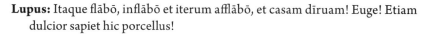

Lupus: Itaque flābō, inflābō et iterum afflābō, et casam dīruam! Euge! Etiam dulcior sapiet hic porcellus!

Nārrātor: Casa dīruitur; porcellus alter ā lupō vorātur. Itaque porcellus tertius structōrī cuidam imperat:

Porcellus Tertius: Salvē, structor. Vīsne mihi laterēs vendere, ut mihi casam construam?

Structor: Libenter hoc faciō!

Nārrātor: Et porcellus tertius sibi casam lateribus construit. Tum, casā lateribus constructā, venit lupus.

Lupus: Porcelle, porcelle, concēde mihi ut in casam ineam!

Porcellus Tertius: Minimē, minimē! Numquam id concēdam.

Lupus: Itaque flābō, inflābō et iterum afflābō, et casam dīruam. Euge! Quam dulcissimus sapiet hic porcellus.

Nārrātor: Lupus flat, inflat et iterum afflat; casa tamen nōn dīruitur.

Lupus: *(sibi)* Dolus mihi fingendus est, quō porcellus ē casā exeat.
   (magnā vōce)
   Porcelle, hortus est mihi nōtus, pōmōrum dulcium plēnus. Vīsne mēcum māne secundā hōrā pōma carpere?

Porcellus Tertius: Libentissimē!

Nārrātor: Porcellus tamen prīmā lūce ad hortum advenit, omnia pōma carpit, ad casam revenit.

Lupus: Porcelle, vīnea est mihi nōta, ūvārum dulcium plēna. Vīsne mēcum māne prīmā lūce ūvās carpere?

Porcellus Tertius: Libentissimē!

Nārrātor: Porcellus tamen ad vīneam ante lūcem advenit, omnēs ūvās carpit, ad casam revenit.

Lupus: Porcelle, sollemne est mihi nōtum. Vīsne mēcum decimā hōrā eō venīre?

Porcellus Tertius: Libentissimē!

Nārrātor: Porcellus tamen ad sollemne prior venit et ad casam revenit. Lupus nunc est īrātissimus.

Lupus: Porcelle, nōn iam potes tē servāre. Nam scālīs sum ascēnsūrus, per tēctum intrātūrus et tē vorātūrus!

Nārrātor: Eō ipsō tempore porcellus cēnam parat. Aēnum in focum pōnit ut lupus in aquam ferventem cadat.

Lupus: Ēheu! ēheu! In aquam ferventem cāsūrus sum!

Porcellus Tertius: Eugepae! Nunc vicissim ego tē vorābō, lupe.

Nārrātor: Et usque ad diēs nostrōs porcellus vītam beātam in casā lateribus cōnstrūctā agit.

Fīnis tortus:

Nārrātor: Eō ipsō tempore advenit Lupus Maximus, quī circum casam volat et lupum in aquam ferventem cāsūrum excipit. Lupus Maximus illum per tēctum ad locum ā casā porcellī remōtissimum portat. Porcellus ex eō tempore vītam beātam in casā lateribus cōnstrūctā agit.

TRĒS PORCELLĪ WORD PLAY
Three Different Huts
In the story, each little pig uses a different building material:

strāmentum, strāmentī, *n., straw, litter*
   used in the **plural**, as a material used for roof coverings:
   strāmenta, strāmentōrum, *n. pl., straw (bundles)*

rāmus, rāmī, *m., branch*

later, lateris, *m., brick, tile*

<u>What form</u> of the word for the building material of each little pig belongs in each sentence? Write the correct form of the appropriate word in the blank provided.

i. Porcellus Tertius "Mihi opus est," inquit, "multīs _____, ut casam validam construam."

ii. "Multa _____ ēmī, ut mihi casam celeriter construam."

iii. Porcellus Alter: "Numerō _____ careō, quibus casam mihi construam."

iv. Porcellus Tertius, _____ ūsus, lupum nōn timet.

v. Vīs _____ et _____ lupō resistere nōn potest.
vīs, vīs, *f., strength, power*

vi. Facillimum est lupō casam _____ constructam flandō dīruere.

vii. Lupus casam alterīus porcellī dērīdet. "_____ nōn timeō; _____ vim flātūs sustinēre nōn possunt."
flātus, flātūs, *m., blast, blowing*

viii. Porcellus Tertius lupum dērīdet. "_____ sunt validī; numquam casam meam dīruere poteris."

8. *Nivea et Septem Nānī*

Vocabulary

accidit, accidere, accidit to happen
adulēscēns, adulēscentis, *m./f.* young person
aeger, aegra, aegrum sick
affectus, -a, -um affected (by) (+ *abl.*)
afferō, afferre, attulī, allātus to bring (toward), bring along
amārus, -a, -um bitter
volus, -a, -um kind, friendly
cantō, cantāre, cantāvī, cantātus to sing; to play music on (+ *abl.*)
capillī, -ōrum, *m. pl.* hair
carmen, carminis, *n.* song
colligō, colligere, collēgī, collectus to gather, pick up
compōnō, compōnere, composuī, compositus to arrange
concēdō, concēdere, concessī, concessūrus to give way, grant, permit
crīnēs, crīnium, *m. pl.* hair
cūrō, cūrāre, cūrāvī, cūrātus to take care of

doceō, docēre, docuī, doctus to teach
doctus, -a, -um learned, wise, taught
dolor, dolōris, *m.* grief, sadness
dōnec, *conj.* until
dormitō, dormitāre, dormitāvī to be sleepy
exitus, -ūs, *m.* end, result
ferus, -ī, *m.* wild beast
glōriōsus, -a, -um boastful, haughty, proud
īdem, eadem, idem the same
incolumis, -e safe and sound, unhurt
inficiō, inficere, infēcī, infectus to poison, taint
īrācundus, -a, -um irritable, wrathful
labellum, -ī, *n.* lip
laetus, -a, -um happy
licet, licēre, licuit + *dat.* it is permitted
lūdō, lūdere, lūsī, lūsus to play

Vocabulary (Continued)

mālum, -ī, *n.* apple
morior, morī, mortuus sum to die
nānus, -ī, *m.* dwarf
niger, nigra, nigrum black
niveus, -a, -um snow-white
nūbō, nūbere, nupsī, nupta (of the woman) to marry
ōlim, *adv.* once (upon a time)
oportet, oportēre, oportuit it is proper
opus, operis, *n.* work, labor
  opus est + *subjunctive* there is need of
ōsculum, -ī, *n.* kiss
palla, -ae, *f.* cloak (worn by women)
pariēs, parietis, *m.* wall
pariō, parere, peperī, partus to bear a child
patella, -ae, *f.* small dish or plate
pavīmentum, -ī, *n.* paved flooring

saevus, -a, -um savage, fierce
sanguineus, -a, -um blood-red
serviō, servīre, servīvī, servītus to serve
silvestris, silvestre of the woods
situs, -a, -um located
speculum, -ī, *n.* mirror
sportella, -ae, *f.* a small basket
sternūtō, sternūtāre, sternutāvī to sneeze (violently)
stultus, -a, -um stupid, foolish
tenuis, tenue weak, feeble
trīstis, -e sad, mournful
valētūdō, valētūdinis, *f.* health
venēnum, -ī, *n.* poison
verrō, verrere to sweep
vīvō, vīvere, vixī, victum to live
vultus, -ūs, *m.* face

Nivea et Septem Nānī

Nārrātor: Vōs laetī ad līberōrum theātrum accipimus. Hodiē vōbīs fābulam dē Niveā et Septem Nānīs agimus. Ōlim rēgīna sīc locūta est:

Rēgīna Prīma: Trīstissima sum. Fīliam dēsīderō, sanguineam labellīs, niveam vultū, nigram capillīs.

Nārrātor: Factum est ita. Rēgīna peperit fīliam, quae Nivea appellāta est. Pulcherrima erat fīliōla. Rēgīna tamen tenuissimā valetūdine erat; mortua est. Rēx, dolōre affectus, rēgīnam alteram glōriōsam, saevam, amāram in mātrimōnium dūxit. Rēgīna altera cotīdiē crīnēs compōnēns sē in speculō spectat et inquit:

Rēgīna Altera: Speculum, speculum in pariete situm, quae fēmina est pulcherrima omnium?

Speculum: Tū, ō rēgīna, pulcherrima omnium es.

Nārrātor: Rēgīna cotīdiē idem quaerit; ūnō tamen diē ...

Rēgīna Altera: Speculum, speculum in pariete situm, quae fēmina est pulcherrima omnium?

Speculum: Tū, ō rēgīna, pulcherrima es, sed Nivea, rēgis fīlia, est pulcherrima omnium quae in rēgnō sunt.

Rēgīna Altera: Vērum nōn dīcis. Pulcherrima omnium ego sum. Opus est ut Nivea statim discēdat. Age, lignātor, Niveam in silvam trahe, et eam in silvā relinque!

Lignātor: Age, Nivea, eāmus in silvam.

Nivea: Libentissimē. In silvā enim flōrēs carpere et cum ferīs lūdere possum.

Nārrātor: In silvā lignātor Niveae casam invenit, et ...

Lignātor: Valē, Nivea. Ego discēdō, tū tamen in casā incolumis manēbis. Sunt septem nānī quī in hāc casā habitant. Benevolī sunt; tē cūrābunt.

Nivea: Quam bella est haec casa! Casa mihi est pūrgenda, patellae lavandae, pavīmentum verrendum, lectī compōnendī. *(ūnā post hōrā)* Dēfessa sum. In hōc lectō cubitum eō.

Nārrātor: Eō ipsō tempore septem nānī ā labōre domum redeunt, carmen cantantēs:

Nānī: Iō, iō, domum ā labōre redeō! Sistite! spectāte! Quid est? Casa pūrgāta est. Quae puella est illa, in lectō dormiēns? Pulcherrima puellula!

Nivea: Salvēte. Mihi nomen est Nivea. Licet mihi in hāc casā vōbīscum habitāre? Quae nōmina vōbīs?

Nānī: Sumus Stultus, Sternutāns, Laetus, Īrācundus, Doctus, Timidus, et Dormitāns. Tibi servīmus. Tē in casam nostram accipimus.

Nivea: Vōs libentissimē salūtō. Vītam beātam nōs omnēs simul agāmus.

Nārrātor: Posthāc Nivea cotīdiē cēnam parat, vestīmenta lavat, casam pūrgat, dum Nānī in silvā labōrant. At quōdam diē rēgīna sē parat et speculō dīcit,

Rēgīna Altera: Speculum, speculum in pariete situm, quae est pulcherrima omnium quae in rēgnō sunt?

Speculum: Tū, ō rēgīna, pulcherrima es, sed Nivea, quae in silvā incolumis habitat, est pulcherrima omnium quae sunt in rēgnō.

Rēgīna Altera: Nivea vīvit! Nōn est possibile! In silvam ībō eam visitātūra. Eī māla venēnō infecta afferam. Nōn oportet Niveam adhūc vīvere!

Nārrātor: Itaque rēgīna, nigrā pallā indūta, quaedam māla colligit, ūnum venēnō īnficit, et omnia in sportellam pōnit ut ea ad casam silvestrem Niveae afferat.

Rēgīna Altera: *(iānuam pulsat)* Salvē, domina. Vīsne mālum dulcissimum edere?

Nivea: Salvē. Libentissimē. Quam dulcia māla!

Nārrātor: Eō ipsō tempore Nivea mālum venēnō infectum edit et ad pavīmentum cadit dormiēns.

Rēgīna Altera: Evax! Nunc rūrsus pulcherrima omnium sum!

Nārrātor: Ūnā post hōrā septem nānī domum redeunt.

Nānī: Iō, iō, domum ā labōre redeō. Sistite! Spectāte! Quid Niveae accidit? Estne aegra? Nōn respondet. In lectō eam pōnāmus et in perpetuum cūrēmus.

Nārrātor: Ita cotīdiē septem nānī Niveam cūrant dōnec ad silvam veniat fīlius rēgis adulēscēns et pulcher.

Fīlius Rēgis: In hāc casā habitat Nivea?

Nānī: Ita vērō, fīlī rēgis, sed nōn respondet. Mortua est.

Fīlius Rēgis: Mortua est? Nōn est possibile! Concēdite mihi ut'eam videam.

Nānī: Ita vērō, fīlī rēgis. Intrā, domine.

Nārrātor: Statim Niveae ōsculum dat fīlius rēgis.

Fīlius Rēgis: Nivea, cārissima, surge!

Nivea: Quid accidit? Quis es?

Fīlius Rēgis: Fīlius rēgis, Nivea, sum. Tē valdē amō. Pulcherrima es omnium quae in rēgnō sunt; tē in mātrimōnium dūcam.

Nivea: Quid septem nānīs accidet?

Fīlius Rēgis: Nānī in rēgiā nōbīscum habitent.

Nānī: Libentissimē! Euge! Laetissimī sumus!

Nārrātor: Omnēs posthāc vītam beātam ēgērunt. Hunc exitum fābula dē Niveā et septem nānīs habet.

Fīnis tortus:

Fīlius Rēgis: Fīlius rēgis, Nivea, sum. Tē valdē amō. Pulcherrima es omnium quae in rēgnō sunt; tē in mātrimōnium dūcam.

Nivea: Minimē! Foedus es; tibi nūbere nōlō. Cum septem nānīs habitō.

Fīlius Rēgis: Nānōs mihi praepōnis?

Nivea: Itā verō, nānōs tibi praepōnō. Cum eīs habitābō.

Nānī: Libentissimē! Euge! Laetissimī sumus!

Nārrātor: Nivea et septem nānī posthāc vītam beātam ēgērunt. Hunc exitum fābula dē Niveā et septem nānīs habet.

Nivea et Septem Nānī Word Play

Translate the following words and phrases from the story into Latin. For nouns and adjectives, use the nominative singular form **unless** the English clue indicates that another form is needed. Then, **find** the Latin words/phrases in the Word Search on page 47.

queen _____

blood-red in lips (with blood-red lips)
   (referring to Nivea) _____

snow-white in face (with a snow-white face)
   (referring to Nivea) _____

black in hair (with black hair)
   (referring to Nivea) _____

of very weak health _____

dead *(referring to Nivea)* _____

mirror _____

on the wall _____

of all _____

woodcutter _____

dwarf _____

safe and sound *(referring to Nivea)* _____

wrathful, bad-tempered
   (referring to one of the dwarfs) _____

poison _____

apple _____

kiss _____

to marry you *(for a man)* _____

to marry you *(for a woman)* _____

NIVEA ET SEPTEM NĀNĪ – 47

marriage _____

to live happily _____

ever after (after this) _____

```
s z o r d v d t e l f e n v z m s d s m
a i b g a x b v r u i e b u e i d o x m
x u l l h c n i e q m i x m l n n h u m
v m t l v p x h g r o d g l l m e n c u
a c h r e e i d a v i v e h i d b n x o
m x a o o b q b m u e p v a f r u t u b
p e s z v m a s a m a t r i m o n i u m
h v c q m v l l t c i o t e d u c e r e
e n i d u t e l a v a m i s s i u n e t
n l p h o d b r e e z i b m m n x c t l
f i f n b u g s b n n s i m u l o c n i
s m v r q i u i m p e i n u a y i n r m
e u r e n n e o a e o t u n p v s o o u
v l d i a v p r t z h p b g t n t s d i
f u i n e v i c i a o a e u n a t c s n
f c o r u e d v s o q r g n a p u v m
s e u a t c h l t u t d e g q i s l u o
c p l e h f a h t v t v i q m a l u m s
b s i c v i a r d u e l g n g b i m b p
d u a a i c a n i g e r g v h d u c m i
```

9. *Fistulātor Versicolor Hamelīnus*

Vocabulary

aedēs, aedium, *f. pl.* house
aliōquī, *adv.* in another way
calamitās, calamitātis, *f.* disaster
cantō, cantāre, cantāvī, cantātus + *abl.* to play an instrument
cantus, -ūs, *m.* song, music
colligō, colligere, collēgī, collectus to gather, pick up
colōnus, -ī, *m.* townsman
consentiō, consentīre, consēnsī, consensus to agree
dēnārius, -ī, *m.* denarius (silver coin)
dissolvō, dissolvere, dissolvī, dissolūtus to resolve
ēvānescō, ēvānescere, ēvānuī to vanish
extrahō, extrahere, extraxī, extractus to remove
fīō, fierī, factus sum to become, to happen
fistula, -ae, *f.* pipe
fistulātor, fistulātōris, *m.* piper
flūvius, -ī, *m.* river
Hamelīnus, -a, -um of the town of Hamelin
Hamelīnum, -ī, *n.* Hamelin
inferō, inferre, intulī, inlātus to bring in
līberī, -ōrum, *m. pl.* children
līberō, līberāre, līberāvī, līberātus to set free
magister, magistrī, *m.* mayor
morbus, -ī, *m.* sickness
mūs, mūris, *m.* rodent, mouse, rat
nūgae, -ārum, *f. pl.* nonsense, idle talk, trifles
opera, -ae, *f.* effort, services
oppidum, -ī, *n.* town
pereō, perīre, periī, peritus to perish
perfidus, -a, -um treacherous, false
postulō, postulāre, postulāvī, postulātus to demand
praeclārē, *adv.* very well
praemium, -ī, *n.* reward
prōpōnō, prōpōnere, prōposuī, prōpositus to offer, set forth
pulex, pulicis, *m.* flea
redimō, redimere, redēmī, redēmptus to ransom

Vocabulary (Continued)

retineō, retinēre, retinuī, retentus to hold onto, detain, restrain

rōdō, rōdere, rōsī, rōsus to gnaw

solvō, solvere, solvī, solūtus to pay

speciēs, speciēī, *f.* appearance

sustineō, sustinēre, sustinuī, sustentus to sustain, endure

taeter, taetra, taetrum hideous, offensive

ubīque, *adv.* everywhere

versicolor, versicolōris parti-colored; of different colors, variegated

Fistulātor Versicolor Hamelīnus

Nārrātor: Salvēte, omnēs. Hodiē vōbīs fābulam dē fistulātōre versicolōre agimus. Fābula est dē oppidō parvō Germānōrum, Hamelīnō nōmine. Huic oppidō calamitātem afferunt mūrēs. Sunt mūrēs plūrimī tōtum per oppidum. Quōdam diē oppidānī ad oppidī magistrum ad calamitātem dissolvendam adveniunt.

Fēmina: Sī vīs, Magister, nōbīs opus est operā tuā. Sunt mūrēs ubīque, omnibus in viīs et imprīmīs omnibus in aedificiīs. Cibum rōdunt; taeterrimī sunt; foedissimā sunt speciē.

Vir: Itā vērō, Magister, tibi est haec rēs dissolvenda. Mūribus sunt pulicēs. Morbōs līberīs nostrīs īnferunt.

Oppidānī: Rem statim dissolve! Mūrēs taeterrimī sunt. Calamitātem sustinēre nōn iam possumus!

Magister: Praeclārē, optimē. Sciō calamitātem dē mūribus esse; praemium sum prōpositūrus cuiquam quī salūtem nōbīs adferat.

Nārrātor: Rē vērā magister praemium prōpōnit: mille dēnāriōs eī solvet quī oppidum mūribus līberāre possit. Posterō diē homō quīdam ad magistrī aedēs accēdit.

Fistulātor: Salvē, Magister. Fistulātor sum versicolor. Fistulā magicā vōs omnēs mūribus līberāre possum.

Magister: *(māgnō rīsū)* Rēs est rīdicula. Fistulātor fistulā magicā omnēs mūrēs ex oppidō extrahās?

Fistulātor: Itā vērō. Sī omnēs mūrēs ex oppidō extrāxerō, mihi praemium solvēs?

Magister: Sīc ut dīcis solvam.

Fistulātor: Optimē. Spatiō ūnīus diēī relictō, nūllī mūrēs in oppidō invenientur.

Nārrātor: Sīc fit, ut dīcit. Cum fistulātor fistulā magicā cantat, tum mūrēs omnēs per viās usque ad flūvium eum sequuntur, et ibi pereunt.

Fistulātor: Optimē! Omnēs mūrēs iam sunt mortuī. Nunc praemium mille dēnāriōrum mihi postulandum est.

Nārrātor: Fistulātor iānuam magistrī pulsat.

Fistulātor: Salvē, Magister. Mūrēs nūllī iam in oppidō sunt. Omnēs extrāxī. Ut praemium mille dēnāriōrum colligam veniō.

Magister: Nōlī nūgās nārrāre! Praemium mille dēnāriōrum numquam solvam magicā fistulā cantātā. Discēde statim ex hōc oppidō; hūc numquam revenī.

Fistulator: Perfidus es, Magister. Mihi praemium aliōquī solvēs.

Nārrātor: Fistulātor versicolor ex magistrī aedibus discēdit; fistulā magicā cantāre incipit. Musica est dulcissima. Cantūs dulcissimī per viās oppidī fluunt. Eō ipsō tempore līberī clāmant:

Puer: Musicam quam dulcissimam audiō! Cantūs sequāmur!

Fistulātor: Venīte, līberī, mēcum venīte. In montēs ambulēmus. Musica vōbīs placet? Sunt plūrēs cantūs dulcissimī in montibus audiendī.

Nārrātor: Itaque līberī fistulātōrem in montēs sequuntur; ex oppidō ēvānescunt. Eā nocte parentēs līberōrum ad magistrī aedēs veniunt et clāmant:

Parentēs: Magister, ubi sunt līberī nostrī? Evānērunt! Ubi est fistulātor versicolor? Is quoque ēvānuit!

Nārrātor: Eō ipsō tempore fistulātor ad magistrī aedēs appāret.

Fistulātor: Līberī in montibus sunt. Cum praemium meritum mihi solveris, līberōs reddam.

Magister: Praemium solvendum est? Quod musicam dulcem cantāvistī?

Fistulātor: Minimē! Praemium solvendum est ut līberōs recipiātis.

Parentēs: Magister, līberī nostrī redimendī sunt! Fistulātōrī praemium solve!

Magister: Itā vērō. Cōnsentiō. Mille dēnāriōs accipe.

Fistulātor: Grātiās tibi, Magister, agō. Crās līberī ad oppidum revenient. Cavē tamen, Magister! Melius est rem solvere et fidem servāre.

Fīnis tortus:

Magister: Praemium numquam solvō. Nam pecūnia nōbīs nūlla est.

Fistulātor: Līberōs igitur in montibus semper retineam, ut in perpetuum saltent.

Nārrātor: Itaque in montibus fistulātor fistulā magicā cantat et līberī saltant, usque ad diēs nostrōs.

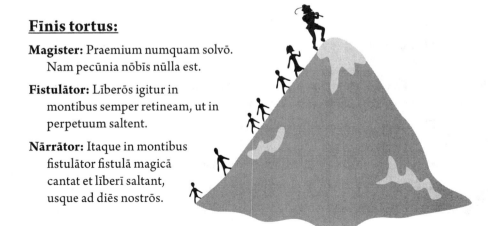

FISTULĀTOR VERSICOLOR HAMELĪNUS WORD PLAY

1. <u>The rats</u>: What form of **mūs, mūris,** *m.,* do you need?

    i. *There are rats everywhere!*

    Sunt _____ ubīque!

    ii. *The rats have fleas!*

    _____ sunt pulicēs!

    iii. *All the buildings are full of rats!*

    Omnia aedificia sunt plēna _____!

    iv. *Can the Pied Piper really remove the rats from the town?*

    Num Fistulātor Versicolor _____ ex oppidō extrahere potest?

    v. *All the citizens of Hamelin are worried about the rats.*

    Omnēs cīvēs Hamelīnī sollicitī dē _____ sunt.

2. <u>Getting rid of the rats</u>: What form of **extrahō, extrahere, extraxī, extractum** do you need?

    i. *The rats must be removed by you, Mayor!*

    Mūrēs tibi, Magister, sunt _____!

    ii. *The rats can never be removed by the Pied Piper, as it seems to the Mayor.*

    Mūrēs ā fistulātōre numquam _____ possunt, ut Magistrō vidētur.

    iii. *The Pied Piper begins to play his magic pipe in order to remove the rats from the town.*

    Fistulātor fistulā magicā cantāre incipit, ut mūrēs ex oppidō _____.

iv. *The Pied Piper has a magic pipe for getting rid of the rats.*
   Fistulātōrī est fistula magica ad mūrēs _____ .

v. *Since the rats have been removed, the Pied Piper is worthy of the reward.*
   Mūribus _____ , Fistulātor praemiō dignus est.
      dignus, -a, -um + *ablative, worthy of*

vi. *If the Piper should get rid of the rats, he would be worthy of the reward.*
   Sī Fistulātor mūrēs _____ , dignus sit praemiō.

vii. *The Piper will be worthy of the prize, if he gets rid of (will have gotten rid of) the rats.*
   Fistulātor erit praemiō dignus, sī mūrēs _____ .

10. *Puella Pulchra Quae Dormiēbat*

Vocabulary

accidit + ut + *subjunctive* it happened that
atrox, atrōcis cruel, horrible
avis, avis, *f.* bird
cārus, -a, -um dear
celebrō, celebrāre, celebrāvī, celebrātus to celebrate
circumdatus, -a, -um surrounded
crūdēlis, crūdēle cruel
dēleō, dēlēre, dēlēvī, dēlētus to destroy
dictū, *supine of dīcere* to say
digitus, -ī, *m.* finger
dūmētum, -ī, *n.* thicket
excēdō, excēdere, excessī to depart from
excitō, excitāre, excitāvī, excitātus to wake up, rouse (+ *someone* in acc.)
forma, -ae, *f.* beauty
fūsus, -ī, *m.* a spindle
horribilis, horribile dreadful
hospes, hospitis, *m./f.* guest
īnfāns, īnfantis, *m./f.* baby

lābor, lābī, lāpsus sum to slip; *(of time)* to pass
lāna, -ae, *f.* wool
lustricus, -a, -um of purification (a ceremony after a birth)
mēnsis, mēnsis, *m.* month
minimus, -a, -um + nātū, *abl. of specification* youngest (in birth)
mors, mortis, *f.* death
mūnus, mūneris, *n.* gift
novem, *indecl. adj.* nine
obdormiscō, obdormiscere, obdormīvī to fall asleep
osculor, osculārī to kiss
pars, partis, *f.* a part
potēns, potentis powerful
praeclārus, -a, -um famous, distinguished, well-known
pretiōsus, -a, -um precious, valuable
quīcumque, quaecumque, quodcumque whoever, whatever
quisnam, quaenam, quidnam who/what, pray tell?

Vocabulary (Continued)

rēgulus, -ī, *m.* petty king; princeling
sagācitās, sagācitātis, *f.* mental acuity
saltātrīx, saltātrīcis, *f.* dancer
somnus, -ī, *m.* sleep
squaleō, squalēre, squaluī to be overgrown from neglect
surgō, surgere, surrēxī, surrectūrus to rise, get up
trahō, trahere, traxī, tractus + lānam to spin wool
venustās, venustātis, *f.* charm, loveliness
veprēs, vepris, *f.* thornbush

Puella Pulchra Quae Dormiēbat

Nārrātor: Hospitēs, vōs ad līberōrum theātrum laetī accipimus. Hodiē vōbīs fābulam agimus dē puellā pulchrā quae dormiēbat. Puella est rēgis fīlia; quōdam diē dīxit rēgīna ...

Rēgīna: Infantem familiae rēgiae dare volō. Māter esse volō!

Nārrātor: Sīc fit, fīliōla pulchra novem post mēnsibus nāta est. Rēgīna igitur inquit,

Rēgīna: Omnēs amīcōs ad diem lustricum celebrandum dēbēmus invītāre.

Rēx: Ita vērō, uxor cāra, et omnēs Nymphās Faunōsque invītēmus.

Nārrātor: Sed nympha potentissima nōn est invītāta. Omnēs amīcī tamen et Nymphae Faunīque omnēs ad epulās adveniunt. Dōna pretiōsissima ad rēgis fīliam afferunt.

Nympha Prīma: Fīliae rēgis sagācitātem dabō.

Nympha Altera: Fīliae rēgis fōrmam mūnerī mittō.

Nympha Tertia: Eī venustātem mūnerī dabō.

Nympha Quarta: Eam mūnere mortis dōnō. Moriētur quīndecim annōs nāta, lānam trahēns.

Omnēs: Horribile dictū! Quam atrōx! quam crūdēle! Nē umquam fīat!

Nārrātor: Nympha tamen minima nātū inquit:

Nympha Quinta: Dōnum meum puellae rēgīnae nōndum datum est. Ecce! Nōn moriētur. Centum annōs dormiet, dōnec rēgulus pulcher eam ōsculō excitet.

Rēx: Ne quis lānam posthāc trahat. Omnēs fūsī deleantur! Morientur omnēs ā quibus lāna trahātur.

Nārrātor: Labuntur annī; fīlia rēgis pulchriōra semper fit. In rēgiā cum parentibus habitat, sed ē rēgiā discēdere eī nōn licet. Quōdam diē partēs rēgiae quam remōtissimās īnspicit. Cubiculum intrat.

Fīlia Rēgis: Salvē, anus. Quidnam facis?

Anus: Lānam trahō, domina. Tū quoque forsitan lānam trahās?

Fīlia Rēgis: Ita vērō, trahere volō!

Nārrātor: Eō ipsō tempore fīlia rēgis digitum fūsō vulnerat; ad pavīmentum cadit dormiēns.

Anus: Ferte auxilium! Fīlia rēgis obdormīvit!

Nārrātor: Eōdem tempore omnēs in rēgiā obdormīvērunt. Etiam canēs dormiunt, fēlēs quoque et avēs. Centum annōs dormit rēgia. Centum post annīs accidit ut rēgulus pulcher per silvam veniat.

Rēgulus: Ecce, rēgia quae procul abest, squalet vepribus et dumētīs circumdata. Ad rēgiam ībō ut quaecumque ibi sint videam.

Nārrātor: Rēgulus ad rēgiam pervenit; intrat et exclāmat:

Rēgulus: Omnēs dormiunt. Ecce, puella rēgia quam pulchra! Pulcherrima omnium, sed mortua vidētur. Eam ōsculābor.

Nārrātor: Eō ipsō tempore, ōsculō datō, ē somnō surgit fīlia rēgis.

Fīlia Rēgis: Quid accidit? Ubi sum? Quis es?

Rēgulus: Fīlius rēgis sum. Puellam tē pulchriōrem numquam vīdī. Tē amō; in mātrimōnium dūcam.

Nārrātor: Omnēs in rēgiā ē somnō iam surgunt. Vītam inde beātam ēgērunt rēgulus et fīlia rēgis.

Fīnis Tortus:

Rēgulus: ... tē in mātrimōnium dūcam.

Fīlia Rēgis: Minimē, Regule. Nēminī nūbam. Rōmam ībō ut saltātrīx praeclāra fīam. Sōla illīc habitābō. Tibi nūbere nōlō.

Nārrātor: Itaque Rēgulus ē rēgnō excēdit; fīlia rēgis quae centum annōs dormiēbat Rōmam it. Vītam inde beātam ēgit et Rēgulus et fīlia rēgis.

Puella Pulchra Quae Dormiēbat Word Play

Match the English meaning with the Latin word:

1. diēs lustricus _____
2. sagācitās _____
3. fōrma _____
4. venustās _____
5. mors _____
6. mūnus _____
7. mūnerī _____
8. fūsus _____
9. lāna _____
10. obdormīre _____
11. ōsculārī _____
12. rēgia _____
13. Nymphae _____
14. Faunī _____

a. wool
b. for a gift
c. purification day
d. to fall asleep
e. beauty
f. a spindle
g. the palace
h. wisdom
i. Sprites
j. a gift
k. charm
l. death
m. to kiss
n. Fairies

Grammar Notes

Auricoma et Ursī Trēs Grammar Notes

Comparison of Adjectives

The adjective **calidus, a, um** means "hot." It is a standard first/second declension or "**us, a, um**" adjective.

To say "hot<u>er</u>" (= the **comparative** degree), we add the suffix **–ior, –ius** to the **base of the adjective:**

> **calidior** *(the masculine and feminine nominative singular),*
>
> **calidius** *(the neuter singular nominative and accusative form)*
>
> The genitive singular (for all three genders) is **calidiōris**.
>
> *(Note that all comparative degree adjectives are third declension.* **Calidiōr-** *is the comparative adjective base to which third declension endings are added:* **calidiōr<u>ī</u>, calidiōr<u>em</u>, calidiōr<u>e</u>,** *etc.)*

We can also translate the comparative as "too hot" or "rather hot."

To say "hot<u>est</u>" (= the **superlative** degree), we add the suffix **–issimus, a, um** to the base of the adjective: **calidissimus, a, um.** *(Note that all superlative degree adjectives are first/second declension.)*

We can also translate the superlative as "very hot, extremely hot."

To exclaim "How hot!" or "This is so hot!," we use **quam** + an adjective: **quam calidus!**

Finding the Base of an Adjective

Remember that the **base of an adjective** (to which we add the comparative suffix **-ior, -ius** and the superlative suffix **-issim-**) is the part of the adjective common to all the positive-degree forms:

calidus, a, um = <u>calid</u>us, <u>calid</u>a, <u>calid</u>um
All three nominatives singular share the base **calid-**.

brevis, -e = <u>brevis</u>, <u>brevis</u>, <u>breve</u>, *brief, short*
All three nominatives share **brev-**.

Both first/second declension adjectives and third declension adjectives also have some words whose masculine nominative singular ends in **-er**:

miser, misera, miserum, *wretched:*   **miser-**

pulcher, pulchra, pulchrum, *beautiful:* **pulchr-**

celer, celeris, celere, *swift:*   **celer-**

ācer, ācris, ācre, *sharp:*   **ācr-**

Note that it is necessary to observe whether the **feminine** and **neuter** keep the **e** of the nominative singular masculine: **mis<u>e</u>ra** (keeps **e**) vs. **pul<u>chr</u>a** (drops **e**), cel<u>e</u>ris vs. ā<u>cr</u>is, etc.

Ablative Absolute

The fourth principal part of the verb is the <u>perfect passive participle</u>:

cōnsūmō, cōnsūmere, cōnsūmpsī, <u>cōnsūmptus</u>, *to eat up, consume.*

The perfect passive participle is a first/second declension adjective that means *"eaten up, consumed."*

It can be used to describe a noun *in the ablative,* to give a quick, shorthand description of what else has happened:

Thus, Auricoma *ate up the porridge,* or **pultem cōnsūmpsit**, a perfect-tense verb governing an accusative direct object, in one sentence, and then she proceeds to do something else in the next sentence—*she goes into the tablīnum* to sit down.

We say that, *when the porridge was eaten up,* or, <u>in shorthand form,</u> *"(with) the porridge consumed,"* **pulte cōnsūmptā**, *she goes to the tablīnum,* **ad tablīnum it**.

Note how the porridge is put into the ablative (**pulte**) and, since it's a feminine noun, it's described by the *feminine ablative form* of the participle (**cōnsūmptā**).

Participle and noun are put into the ablative to show that they are only connected rather loosely (in terms of grammar) to the rest of the sentence. The porridge is **not** the subject (nominative) or the direct object (accusative) in this sentence: in effect, it is in the *ablative* precisely to show that it is more or less *in the background* ("attendant circumstances") in this sentence. The name for this participial construction is ablative absolute.

Latin does not have a perfect active participle (for regular verbs): English might easily say, *Having eaten the porridge, she goes into the tablinum,* where the active participle ("Having eaten") modifies Goldilocks, and in Latin terms would be put into the nominative.

Since Latin has only the perfect passive participle to work with, note that it's the *thing consumed,* **the porridge**, that is described by the perfect passive participle; and to say this as briefly and economically as possible, both noun and participle are put into the ablative: **pulte cōnsūmptā**.

Some people like to use the translation "with the porridge consumed," to help reflect that the words are in the ablative case. "The porridge having been consumed" is another way to reflect that **cōnsūmptā** is perfect and passive. Others feel that these sound too much like "Latin class translationese." More idiomatic translations in English, using subordinate clauses instead of participles, would include "**when** the porridge had been consumed" or "**after** she had consumed the porridge." In any case, we must remember that the participle in Latin describes the porridge, not Goldilocks herself.

PALLIOLĀTELLA GRAMMAR NOTES
Comparison of Adverbs
Just as adjectives are either **positive**, **comparative**, or **superlative** in degree, so also are adverbs:

celeriter, *quick* **celerius,** *quicker* **celerrimē,** *quickest*

Many positive adverbs are formed from adjectives:

Third declension adjectives (**celer, celeris, celere,** *quick*) add **–iter** to the base to form the adverb (**celeriter,** *quickly*); first/second declension adjectives (**lentus, a, um,** *slow*) add **–ē** to the base (**lentē,** *slowly*).

The comparative-degree adverb is identical to the neuter nominative/accusative singular comparative-degree adjective: both forms end in **–ius** (added to the adjective's base)

lentē, *slowly* **lentius,** *more slowly*

prope, *near* **propius,** *nearer, closer*

The superlative-degree adverb ends in **–ē**, with superlative suffix (e.g., **–issim–** or **–rim–**), since all superlative adjectives are first/second declension adjectives (which add **–ē** to form adverbs).

lentissimus, a, um, *most slow* **lentissimē,** *most slowly*

celerrimus, a, um, *most swift* **celerrimē,** *most swiftly*

Remember that the **–er** adjectives of both declensions form the superlatives by adding the suffix **–rimus** to the nominative masculine singular form:

ācer, ācris, ācre, *sharp, keen* superlative **ācerrimus, a, um,** *most sharp, keenest* (but comparative degree is made, as usual, from the base of the positive degree: **ācrior, ācrius,** *sharper*)

The forms of the adverbs that are made from **ācer** are as follows:

positive **ācriter,** *keenly*; comparative **ācrius,** *more keenly*; superlative **ācerrimē,** *most keenly*

Purpose Clause

Latin uses **a subordinate clause** (never *an infinitive phrase*, as in English, e.g., "she runs away <u>to hide</u>" or "... in order <u>to hide</u>") to express the reason <u>why someone does something</u> (= ***a purpose***).

Latin uses the equivalent of "she runs away <u>in order that she (may) hide</u>."

The verb in a Latin purpose clause must be a **subjunctive** form. **The subjunctive** is used to express actions that may happen **hypothetically**, or to indicate what the speaker **is wishing for**. Contrast *the indicative verb*, which expresses *factual actions*:

<u>indicative</u>

pluit, *it's raining* (factual)

<u>subjunctive</u>

pluat, *it may rain* (hypothetical, potential); *let it rain!* (wish)

sī pluat, *if it should rain* (conditional)

The <u>present active subjuntive</u> is formed by adding the vowel **–e–** or **–a–** and the subjunctive *personal endings* (**–m**, **–s**, **–t**, **–mus**, **–tis**, **–nt**) to the present stem. Verbs of the first conjugation use **–e–** as the stem vowel; all other conjugations use **–a–**. Because some present stems end in a vowel, some subjunctive forms contain two vowels immediately before the personal ending.

	Singular	**Plural**	**Conjugation**	**Vowel(s)**
First person	am**em**	am**ēmus**	First conj.	–e–
Second person	am**ēs**	am**ētis**		
Third person	am**et**	am**ent**		
First person	vide**am**	vide**āmus**	Second conj.	–ea–
Second person	vide**ās**	vide**ātis**		
Third person	vide**at**	vide**ant**		
First person	dūc**am**	dūc**āmus**	Third conj.	–a–
Second person	dūc**ās**	dūc**ātis**		
Third person	dūc**at**	dūc**ant**		
First person	iaci**am**	iaci**āmus**	Third –io conj.	–ia–
Second person	iaci**ās**	iaci**ātis**		
Third person	iaci**at**	iaci**ant**		
First person	dormi**am**	dormi**āmus**	Fourth conj.	–ia–
Second person	dormi**ās**	dormi**ātis**		
Third person	dormi**at**	dormi**ant**		

For the <u>passive</u> present subjunctive, add the **passive personal endings** (**-r, -ris, -tur, -mur, -minī, -ntur**).

A <u>positive</u> purpose clause starts with the conjunction **ut** (= *in order that, so that*); a <u>negative</u> purpose clause starts with **nē** (= *in order that... not, lest*).

Deponent Verbs

Some verbs have forms that **look passive**, but are translated with **active meanings**. It will be clear from the principal parts, which are *all passive*, that it is a deponent verb:

loquor, loquī, locūtus sum, *to speak*: This is a deponent third conjugation verb; compare **loquī** with the pres. pass. infin. (**dūcī**) of the third conjugation **dūcō, dūcere, dūxī, ductus**.

Third singular indicative forms:

Present	**loquitur**
Imperfect	**loquēbātur**
Future	**loquētur**
Perfect	**locūtus est**
Pluperfect	**locūtus erat**
Future perfect	**locūtus erit**

Note that the perfect participle of a deponent verb is <u>active</u> in meaning:

locūtus, a, um, *having spoken*

The imperatives:

singular: **loquere!**, *speak!*

(N.B.: This form looks like a present active infinitive; because **loquor** is deponent and thus does not have active forms, **loquere** can only be the imperative.)

plural: **loquiminī!**, *speak!*

(N.B.: This form is identical to the second person plural indicative form of deponent verbs. Use the context of the story to determine the meaning.)

Cinerellula Grammar Notes

Hortatory Subjunctive

In addition to their use in purpose clauses ("... in order that she may hide"), subjunctive verb forms can be used as **main verbs** to express a sort of wish, a command of the "Let's do it!" variety, where the speaker includes him- or herself in the wished-for action.

ambulāre, *to walk*	**Ambulēmus!,** *Let's walk!*
vidēre, *to see*	**Videāmus!,** *Let's see!*
dīcere, *to say*	**Dīcāmus!,** *Let's say!*
diem dīcere, *to set a date*	**Diem dīcāmus!,** *Let's set the date!*

This is called the **hortatory subjunctive**, from the deponent verb **hortor, hortārī, hortātus sum,** *to encourage, exhort.*

A similar usage is called the **jussive subjunctive** (from the verb **iubeō, iubēre, iussī, iussum,** *to order*); note that the speaker wishes that someone else (neither the speaker nor the person whom the speaker addresses) will perform an action.

venīre, *to come*	**Veniat!,** *Let him/her come!*
	Veniant!, *Let them come!*

A **prohibition** (or negative command) can be issued using **nē** + subjunctive; in classical prose, it is **nē** + *perfect* subjunctive, but **nē** + *present* subjunctive, as in **nē sīs,** "don't be," is common in the early comic writer Plautus, and has been used here.

Gerundive + *Sum* (Passive Periphrastic)

Any form of the verb **esse,** "to be," can be combined with a verb's **gerundive** to express an **obligation** ("must be done," "has to be done," etc.):

Hoc est faciendum.	*This **is to-be-done**, or This must be done.*
Haec sunt facienda.	*These things must be done.*
Haec epistula erat scrībenda.	*This letter **was to-be-written**, or had to be written.*

With this construction, a noun or pronoun in the **dative** expresses the **agent**:

Liber <u>mihi</u> scrībendus erit. *I will have to write the book.*
 (The book **will have *to-be-written*** by me.)

Note that the form of **esse**, "to be," determines the tense (and also mood, i.e., indicative, infinitive, or subjunctive) of the expression of obligation.

The **gerundive**, also called the *future passive participle*, is formed from the present stem of the verb (all –**iō** verbs add an **i** to the present stem):

amāre, *to love*	**amandus, a, um,** *to be loved*
vidēre, *to see*	**videndus, a, um,** *to be seen*
dūcere, *to lead*	**dūcendus, a, um,** *to be led*
iaciō, iacere, *to throw*	**iaciendus, a, um,** *to be thrown*
audīre, *to hear*	**audiendus, a, um,** *to be heard*

Double Dative

In certain set phrases, a noun (often an abstract noun) is put into the **dative** (*dative of purpose*) and combined with the dative form of a person (*dative of reference*):

Hoc <u>mihi</u> <u>cordī</u> est. *This is dear to me.*
 cor, cordis, *n., heart*

Haec <u>tibi</u> <u>odiō</u> sunt. *These things are hateful to you.*
 odium, -ī, *n., hatred*

Omnia <u>eīs</u> sunt <u>ūsuī</u>. *All things are useful to them.*
 ūsus, -ūs, *m., use*

Quid est <u>auxiliō</u> <u>vōbīs</u>? *What is helpful to you all?*
 auxilium, -ī, *n., help, assistance*

Note that, in our English translation, the Latin noun in the dative of purpose is likely to be translated by an adjective:

Hoc mihi cordī est. *This is <u>dear</u> to me.*
 (not the more literal *This is <u>for my heart</u>.*)

GALLĪNA RŪFA GRAMMAR NOTES
Ad + Gerundive to Express Purpose

Another use of the **gerundive**, or *future passive participle*, is in the accusative case following the preposition **ad**, in the meaning "for (the purpose of), to."

Ad governs an accusative-case noun, which is modified by the gerundive:

edere, *to eat*
pānis, pānis, *m., bread*   "to eat bread":   **ad pānem edendum**

scrībere, *to write*
epistula, -ae, *f., letter*   "to write letters," "for writing letters":   **ad epistulās scrībendās**

redimere, *to redeem*
captīvus, -ī, *m., prisoner*   "to redeem captives":   **ad captīvōs redimendōs**

faciō, facere, *to make*
poēma, poēmatis, *n., poem*   "to make a poem":   **ad poēma faciendum**

Observe that the gender and number of the accusative-case noun governed by **ad** controls the form of the gerundive used. As with all adjectives and participles, the gerundive agrees with the noun it modifies in gender, number, and case; the endings of the noun and the gerundive may be different from each other depending on the declension of the noun.

"to make poems":   **ad poēmata facienda**

Notice that, to translate this type of phrase in English, we use an **active-voice** translation, although the gerundive in Latin is actually passive:

edendus, a, um means "to be eaten"; "for bread to be eaten" is not idiomatic in English, so we replace it with the active-voice translation:

"for eating bread, to eat bread":   **ad pānem edendum**

Homunculus Condītus Grammar Notes
"As ____ As Possible"
quam + the superlative adjective or adverb means "as ____ as possible," or "to the highest degree possible."

So, for example, the Gingerbread Man (or **Homunculus Condītus**) can taunt the people and animals he flees from by saying, "Run as fast as ever you can, you can't eat me":

Currite, currite <u>quam celerrimē</u> potestis! Mē edere nōn potestis!

Even with the form of **possum** omitted, **quam celerrimē** means "as fast as possible."

Common with adverbs, the idiom exists also with adjectives:

The wicked queen in the story of Snow White (or **Nivea**) might expect to be considered **quam pulcherrima**, "the most beautiful woman possible."

Participles of The Verb *Īre* (And Its Compounds)
Eō, īre, iī, "to go," and its compounds, such as **trānseō, trānsīre,** "to go across," and **ineō, inīre,** "to go into, to enter," have gerundives and present participles that are slightly irregular:

trānseundus, a, um, "to be crossed, to be gone over"

trānsiēns, trānseuntis, "crossing over"

In the story, the **Homunculus Condītus** will be caught by his pursuers, unless he can cross the stream: "**Rīvus tibi trānseundus est**," "you must cross the stream," as the fox points out to him. Literally, "The stream must be crossed by you."

Notice that **trānsīre**, "to cross (over)," can be used transitively (i.e., **transīre** can take a direct object).

But noncompounded **eō, īre,** "to go," is an intransitive verb (i.e., **eō** cannot take a direct obect); thus, the only gerundive form belonging to **īre** is the neuter **eundum**, which can be used in an <u>impersonal</u> gerundive + **sum** expression like **Mihi eundum est**, "I must go" (literally, "it must be gone by me").

TRĒS HIRCĪ ASPERĪ GRAMMAR NOTES

Active Periphrastic

The **future active participle** can be combined with any form of the verb **esse,** "to be," to produce a two-word (or "roundabout," i.e., **periphrastic**) equivalent of the future tense. This can be compared to the "near future" structure in English: "he <u>is going to go</u>" versus the simple future indicative "he <u>will go</u>."

The future active participle is easily formed by adding the suffix **–ūrus, a, um** to the participial stem (or supine stem) of the verb; this is the stem of the active verb's fourth principal part, or of the deponent verb's third principal part:

principal parts of verb	*participial stem*	*future active participle*
dīcō, dīcere, dīxī, dictus, *to say*	dict–	**dictūrus, a, um,** *about to say, intending to say*
conor, conārī, conātus sum, *to try*	conāt–	**conātūrus, a, um,** *about to try, intending to try*

In the story, the fierce gnome (or **faunus trux**) living under the bridge threatens to climb up and eat the goat that's making so much noise:

Ego <u>sum ascensūrus</u> ut tē confestim vorem.

Notice that the future active participle (in the accusative case) plus the infinitive form of **esse,** "to be," are combined to make the future active infinitive used in indirect statement:

The fierce gnome says that he <u>will climb up</u> in order to eat the goat.
Faunus trux dīcit sē <u>ascensūrum esse</u> ut hircum voret.

Ablative of Comparison

There are two ways of making a comparison between two people or things, using the comparative degree (e.g., "faster," "bigger") of an adverb or adjective.

(1) Use **quam**, "than," and keep both members of the comparison *in the same case:*

    Frāter meus celerius currit <u>quam tū</u>.   *My brother runs faster than you.*

    Since **frāter** is nominative, the second member, **tū,** is also nominative, following **quam**.

(2) Put the *second member* of the comparison into the *ablative case:*

    Frāter meus celerius <u>tē</u> currit.   *My brother runs faster than you.*

    Quam is not used here. The second member is put into the ablative: **tē**.

TRĒS PORCELLĪ GRAMMAR NOTES
Indirect Command
Another subordinate-clause use of the subjunctive is in a clause that serves as the object of certain verbs that mean "to order" or "command." They resemble purpose clauses, in that positive commands are introduced by the conjunction **ut**, and negative commands by **nē** (and because their verbs also are **prospective**, i.e., anticipate a **future** action):

I order them <u>to attack</u> the city.   (English uses the infinitive.)

*I order them <u>that they should attack</u>
  the city.*   (rendered as a subordinate
    clause, in English)

Eīs imperō <u>ut urbem oppugnent</u>.   **oppugnāre**, "to attack"

I ask you <u>not to leave</u> the city.

I ask <u>that you not leave</u> the city.

Tē ōrō <u>nē ab urbe discēdās</u>.   **discēdere**, "to leave (from)"

Some verbs (like **imperāre**) require a **dative** (**eīs**) of the person asked; others, like **ōrāre**, require an **accusative** (**tē**).

Like **imperāre** in requiring a dative are **mandāre, praecipere, persuādēre, concēdere**; like **ōrāre** in requiring an accusative are **rogāre, obsecrāre, hortārī, impellere**. There are also some verbs that require **ā / ab** + **ablative** *("to seek from a person")*: **petere, postulāre, impetrāre**.

Still other verbs, such as **iubēre**, have a completely different construction: they are followed by an **accusative / infinitive clause**, as in English:

I order <u>them to attack</u> the city.
<u>Eōs</u> iubeō urbem <u>oppugnāre</u>.

Similar to **iubēre** in structure are **sinere** and **patī** ("to allow"), and **vetāre** and **prohibēre** ("to forbid").

Nivea et Septem Nānī Grammar Notes

Ablative of Respect

The ablative can be used with adjectives like "worthy" (**dignus, a, um**), or descriptive adjectives ("beautiful," **pulcher, pulchra, pulchrum**) to **limit** or **identify the respect** in which the adjective is true:

He is worthy of praise.
Dignus est laude.

You are beautiful in appearance.
Tū es fōrmā pulchra.

In the story, Snow White's (or **Nivea's**) mother has a specific type of baby girl in mind:

"blood-red in lips, snow-white in face, black in hair."

In Latin, the **ablative case** will be used to limit or define *the respect in which* the baby will be blood-red, snow-white, and black, where English uses a prepositional phrase:

sanguineam labellīs, niveam vultū, nigram capillīs.

The use of ablative **nātū** ("in birth") is common with the adjectives **maior** ("older") and **minor** ("younger").

Ablative of Description

A two-word **phrase** (adjective + noun) in the **ablative case** may be used to give a description of the appearance or dress of a person:

Est puella sanguineīs labellīs, niveō vultū, nigrīs capillīs.
She is a girl with blood-red lips, snow-white face, black hair.

If you compare the two "Snow White" descriptions above, you will see that the first one given under "Ablative of Respect" has ablative nouns (**labellīs, vultū, capillīs**), one for each feminine accusative singular (**–am**) adjective; the adjectives are describing **fīliam** (understood), object of **dēsīderō** ("I want").

In the second description, however, there are two-word ablative phrases (**sanguineīs labellīs**, etc.), where the adjective (**sanguineīs**) directly describes the (ablative) lips (**labellīs**); the whole phrase, adjective and noun in the ablative, describes the girl.

Partitive Genitive with Superlative Adjectives

When a superlative adjective is used (**pulcherrima,** "most beautiful"), a partitive genitive expressing the whole group that the individual is being compared with (**omnium,** "of all") may be added.

bravest <u>of the soldiers</u>: **fortissimus <u>mīlitum</u>**

smallest <u>of the children</u>: **minimus <u>līberōrum</u>**

Fistulator Versicolor Hamelinus Grammar Notes

Opus Est Constructions

The noun **opus, operis,** *n.*, means "work, labor." It is also used in the phrase **opus est**, which is equivalent to **necesse est** ("there is need, it is necessary").

> **Opus est** may be followed by <u>an ablative of the thing needed</u>:
>
> In the story, one of the citizens of Hamelin tells the Mayor (or **Magister**),
>
> > **Opus est <u>operā tuā</u>!** *There is need of <u>your efforts/exertion</u>!*
>
> **Opus est** may also be followed by <u>an infinitive</u>
>
> > **Opus est urbem mūribus <u>līberāre</u>,** *It is necessary <u>to rid</u> the city of rats,*
>
> or by an <u>ut + subjunctive clause</u>.
>
> In the story of Snow White (or **Nivea**), the jealous Queen, wanting to remain the most beautiful of all, said
>
> > **Opus est <u>ut Nivea statim discēdat</u>,** *It's necessary <u>for Nivea to leave immediately</u>;*
>
> and then she sent for the Woodsman (Lignātor) to take the girl away.

Potential Subjunctive

Like the **hortatory** and **jussive** subjunctives, which express *wishes* (**Let's go!**, *hortatory*; **Let them go!**, *jussive*), the **potential subjunctive** is a main-verb subjunctive that expresses <u>a possibility</u>. (Contrast the **indicative**, which expresses <u>a fact</u>.)

> In the story, the Mayor is openly contemptuous of the idea that the Piper (**Fistulātor**) can rid the town of rats using his magic pipe:
>
> > **Fistulātor fistulā magicā omnēs mūrēs ex oppidō <u>extrahās</u>?**
> > *You, a piper, <u>could remove</u> all the rats from the town with a magic pipe?*
>
> Contrast the indicatives: **extrahis,** *you are removing*; **extrahēs,** *you will remove,* etc. (factual statements) with **extrahās** (a possibility).

PUELLA PULCHRA QUAE DORMIĒBAT GRAMMAR NOTES

Gift-Giving

This is a story that concerns gift-giving; it seemed appropriate to consider some of the various ways the act of gift-giving can be expressed in Latin.

Note that there are two common words for gift:

dōnum, -ī, *n., gift* (from the same stem as the verb **dō, dare, dedī, datus**)

mūnus, mūneris, *n., gift* (with broader range of meanings, including "service, function")

The verb **dō, dare, dedī, datus**, "to give," governs an <u>accusative</u> of the thing given and a <u>dative</u> of the person to whom the gift is given:

The first fairy (or **Nympha Prima**) says,

"I will give the king's daughter wisdom."
Fīliae rēgis sagācitātem dabō.

Or we can use the same verb, **dare**, governing an accusative (direct object) and a dative (indirect object) as before, but with a <u>dative of purpose</u>, **dōnō**, "for a gift," added as well:

The third fairy (**Nympha Tertia**) says,

"I will give charm to her <u>as a present</u>."
Eī venustātem <u>dōnō</u> dabō.

There is also the related verb **dōnō, dōnāre, dōnāvī, dōnātus**, "to present someone (accusative) with a gift (ablative)":

The **Nympha Quarta**, the one who had not been invited, says,

"I present her with the gift of death:"
Eam mūnere mortis dōnō.

Notice that this verb, **dōnāre**, governs an <u>accusative of the person</u> (= the recipient), and an <u>ablative</u> (of means / instrument) <u>for the present</u> itself.

It is also possible to use **mittō, mittere, mīsī, missus,** "to send," governing an accusative of the gift, plus the noun **mūnus** in the dative (purpose) and a dative for the recipient (indirect object):

The second fairy (**Nympha Altera**) announces,

"I'm sending the king's daughter beauty as a gift."
Fīliae rēgis fōrmam mūnerī mittō.

Grammar Exercises

Auricoma et Ursī Trēs Grammar Exercises

I. *Quid facit puella? / Quid fēcit puella?*

Using the principal parts given, (a) change the underlined verbs from **present** tense to the corresponding form of the **perfect**; then (b) express the first action in the sentence using **an ablative absolute**.

1. Auricoma iānuam <u>aperit</u> et in casam <u>intrat</u>.
   aperiō, aperīre, aperuī, apertus; intrō, intrāre, intrāvī, intrātus

   a. Auricoma iānuam _____ et in casam _____.

   b. Auricoma, _____ _____, in casam _____.

2. Puella sellam minimam <u>probat</u> et in eā <u>sedet</u>.
   probō, probāre, probāvī, probātus; sedeō, sedēre, sēdī

   a. Puella sellam minimam _____ et in eā _____.

   b. _____ _____ _____, puella _____.

   NB: *The prepositional phrase **in eā** is not needed with the ablative absolute construction.*

3. Eheu! Puella gravior sellam minimam <u>frangit</u>, et in solum <u>cadit</u>!
   frangō, frangere, frēgī, fractus; cadō, cadere, cecidī

   a. Eheu! Puella gravior sellam minimam _____, et in solum _____!

   b. Eheu! _____ _____ _____, puella gravior in solum _____!

4. Ursī puellam in lectō Ursulī <u>inveniunt</u>, et <u>exclāmant</u>.
   inveniō, invenīre, invēnī, inventus; exclāmō, exclāmāre, exclāmāvī, exclāmātus

   a. Ursī puellam in lectō Ursulī _____, et _____.

   b. _____ in lectō Ursulī _____, Ursī _____.

II. *Auricoma cibōs variōs probat*

In the story, Auricoma tries the porridge (**puls, pultis,** f.) that Ursa Mater has made for the family:

> "Haec puls est optima!"
> Et omnem pultem cōnsūmpsit.
> Tum, pulte cōnsūmptā, Auricoma ad tablīnum it, . . .

Suppose that, instead of porridge, Auricoma had eaten a different food; **how would the underlined adjectives** in the passage above, which describe the (feminine singular) porridge, **have to change?** Write the changed Latin sentences in the space provided.

The first one is done for you as a model:

1. **mel, mellis,** *n. honey*

   > "<u>Hoc mel</u> est optimum!"
   > Et <u>omne mel</u> cōnsūmpsit.
   > Tum, <u>melle cōnsūmptō</u>, Auricoma ad tablīnum it, . . .

   "<u>This honey</u> is <u>excellent</u>!"
   And she ate up <u>all the honey</u>.
   Then, <u>when the honey has been eaten</u>, Auricoma goes to the study, . . .

2. **mālum, mālī,** *n. apple*
   (Use the plural: "These apples")

3. **glans, glandis,** *m. acorn*
   (Use the singular: "The food" from the nuts)

4. **brassica, brassicae,** *f. cabbage*

5. **ūva, ūvae,** *f. grape*
   (Use the plural: "These grapes")

III. *Maximum, Mediocre, Minimum?* Which Is Better?

1. Imagine that Auricoma is discussing the different bowls of porridge with the Ursī Trēs. Use the appropriate forms of **hic, haec, hoc** ("this one") and **mediocris, mediocris, mediocre** ("medium-sized") to complete the sentences.

    a. Tibi placet ista patella minima; Ursō Patrī placet illa patella maxima; sed mihi placet _____ patella _____.

    b. Age, Ursule, istam patellam minimam lavā! Lavā quoque patellam patris, illam maximam! Ego _____ patellam _____ lavābō.

2. Naturally, the Ursī Trēs have distinctive goblets, in the three appropriate sizes: biggest for Father, medium for Mother, smallest for Baby Bear.

    Use the word **pōculum, pōculī,** *n., cup, goblet,* with a demonstrative adjective of your choice—"this one" (a form of **hic**), "that one of yours" (a form of **iste**), "that one over there" (a form of **ille**)—and the **appropriate size words**:

    Ursus Pater _____ pōculum _____ haurit.

    Ursae Matrī est _____ pōculum _____.

    Eheu! _____ pōculum _____ dē manibus Ursulī cadit!

Palliolātella Grammar Exercises

I. Purpose Clauses

In the following exercise, explain why each character does something, using a purpose clause to complete the Latin sentence. Use the underlined portion of the English sentence and the Latin vocabulary words to help you.

The first one is done as a model:

1. The wolf uses tricks <u>in order to catch Little Red Riding Hood and eat her up</u>.
    *(in order that **he may catch** her and **eat** her **up**)*

    Lupus dolīs ūtitur <u>ut Palliolātellam corripiat et edat</u>.

    > ūtor, ūtī, ūsus sum, *to use* + ablative (of means) as object
    > dolus, -ī, *m. trick*
    > corripiō, corripere, corripuī, correptus, *to catch*
    > edō, edere, ēdī, ēsus, *to eat (up)*

2. The mother sends food and medicine <u>in order to help the grandmother</u>.
    *(in order that **she may help** the grandmother)*

    Māter cibum et medicāmina mittit _____.

    > adiuvō, adiuvāre, adiūvī, adiūtus, *to help*
    > avia, -ae, *f. grandmother*

3. The woodcutter wields his ax <u>in order to save Little Red Riding Hood and the grandmother</u>.
    *(in order that **he may save** ...)*

    Lignātor dolabrā ūtitur _____.

    > servō, servāre, servāvī, servātus, *to save*

4. Little Red Riding Hood picks beautiful flowers <u>in order to please grandmother</u>.
    *(in order that **she may please** ...)*

    Palliolātella flōrēs pulchrōs carpit _____.

    > placeō, placēre, placuī, + dative, *to please (someone)*

5. *Grandmother hides <u>in order that she not be killed by the wolf</u>.*
   (lest **she be killed** ... / in order that **she not be killed** ...)

   Avia sē cēlat _____.

   interficiō, interficere, interfēcī, interfectus, *to kill*

II. Deponent Verbs

Many deponent verbs are equivalent in meaning to "regular" verbs.

Review the forms of the "regular" verbs by comparing them to forms of deponent verbs:

1. Match Meanings: Given the ***deponent verb's infinitive*** and ***translation***, <u>find</u> the <u>infinitive of the verb that matches in meaning</u>. Write the letter for the "regular" verb in the blank next to the corresponding deponent verb.

i.	loquī, *to speak*	_____	a.	temptāre
ii.	proficīscī, *to leave*	_____	b.	dīcere
iii.	ingredī, *to enter*	_____	c.	manēre
iv.	regredī, *to return*	_____	d.	intrāre
v.	morārī, *to stay*	_____	e.	discēdere
vi.	conārī, *to try*	_____	f.	redīre

2. Match Forms: Match forms of the deponent verbs **morārī** and **loquī** to the forms of the "regular" verbs **manēre** and **dīcere** that correspond in meaning. Look for verb forms that have the same person, number, voice, mood, and tense. Write the letter for the "regular" verb in the blank next to the deponent verb.

deponent form   *"regular" verb form*

i.   morātus es   _____   a. mānserint
ii.   loquuntur   _____   b. dīcēbat
iii. morāberis   _____   c. manēbāmus
iv.   loquentur   _____   d. dīxeris
v.   morābāmur   _____   e. mānsistī
vi.   locūta erat   _____   f. dīcent
vii. morātī erunt   _____   g. maneō
viii. locūtae estis   _____   h. dīcunt
ix.   moror   _____   i. mānserāmus
x.   loquēbātur   _____   j. dīxistis
xi.   morātae erāmus   _____   k. manēbis
xii. locūtus eris   _____   l. dīxerat

Cinerellula Grammar Exercises

I. The Hortatory Subjunctive

For the following exercise, imagine that you are the speaker. Using the hortatory subjunctive (e.g., "**Let's play** ball!"), how would you suggest in Latin the activity indicated in the English sentence?

1. Baby Bear suggests to Goldilocks that they play ball:

    lūdō, lūdere, lūsī, lūsus, *to play*, + *ablative* (pila, -ae, *f. ball*):

    Age, Auricoma, _____!

2. Little Red Riding Hood suggests to her friends that they pluck flowers:

    carpō, carpere, carpsī, carptus, *to pluck*
    flōs, flōris, *m. flower*

    Agite, amīcae, _____!

3. Mother Bear suggests to Baby Bear and Goldilocks that they wash the dishes:

    lavō, lavāre, lāvī, lautus/lavātus *to wash*
    patella, -ae, *f. dish, bowl*

    Agite, līberī, _____!

4. One wicked stepsister suggests to the other that they torment Cinderella:

    cruciō, cruciāre, cruciāvī, cruciātus, *to torture, torment*
    Cinerellula, -ae, *f. Cinderella*

    Age, soror, _____!

5. The stepmother suggests to her daughters that they get ready for the ball:

    sē parāre, *to get ready* (mē parō, tē parās, nōs parāmus, *etc., in the indicative mood*)
    ad epulās, *for the ball*

    Agite, fīliae meae, _____!

II. Passive Periphrastic = Gerundive + *sum*

Rewrite the following Latin sentences to express <u>what must be done</u> using the passive periphrastic construction rather than the **dēbēre** construction; remember that the "agent" (the person who will do the action) is put into the **dative**.

Model: Cinerellula "**Patrōna** Faunōrum haec omnia **dēbet** facere," ait.
    Cinerellula "**Haec omnia** Patrōnae Faunōrum **facienda sunt!**" ait.

1. Ursī Trēs pultem edere dēbent.

    puls, pultis, *f.*

    Puls _____ .

2. Gallīna rūfa sōla pānem edere dēbet.

    pānis, pānis, *m.*

    Pānis _____ .

3. Omnēs gallīnam rūfam adiuvāre dēbent.

    Gallīna rūfa _____ .

4. "Nōs puellam pulchram quaerere dēbēmus."

    "Puella pulchra _____ ."

5. "Omnēs lectōs probāre dēbeō," inquit Auricoma.

    "Omnēs lectī _____ ."

6. Patrōna Faunōrum omnia magicā arte trānsformāre dēbet.

    Omnia _____ .

III. Double Datives

Who would say the following? Find the speaker; translate each statement. Write the letter for the character in the blank next to the corresponding statement. Write out the translation in the space below the statement.

i. "Cinerellula mihi odiō est." _____

ii. "Ego Palliolātellae et aviae salūtī erō." _____

iii. "Palliolātella mihi cūrae est." _____

iv. "Puella pulchra mihi cordī est." _____

v. "Eheu! Lignātor mihi exitiō erit!" _____

vi. "Cucurbita et mūrēs nōbīs ūsuī erunt." _____

vii. "Gallīna rūfa vōbīs exemplō sit." _____

Choices:
a. Patrōna Faunōrum
b. Nārrātor
c. Lupus
d. Lignātor
e. Noverca
f. Māter
g. Fīlius rēgis

GALLĪNA RŪFA GRAMMAR EXERCISES

I. Expressing Purpose

In addition to the <u>purpose clause</u> (= **ut** / **nē** + subjunctive), we may use **ad + the gerund** or <u>gerundive</u> (in the accusative) to express **the reason why someone does something**.

Use the appropriate vocabulary (given here) to form (a) a purpose clause and (b) an ad + gerundive phrase.

1. *Goldilocks grabs the smallest bowl, <u>in order to eat up the porridge</u>.*
   (in order that she may eat up ...)

   puls, pultis, *f. porridge*
   cōnsūmō, cōnsūmere, cōnsumpsī,
      cōnsumptus, *to eat up, to consume*

   a. Auricoma patellam minimam corripit, ut _____.

      cōnsūmere gives us the gerundive _____ -us, -a, -um, "*to be eaten up, to be consumed*"

   b. Auricoma patellam minimam corripit ad _____.

2. *Little Red Riding Hood goes into the woods <u>in order to pick flowers</u>.*
   (in order that she may pick ...)

   flōs, flōris, *m. flower*
   carpō, carpere, carpsī, carptus, *to pick*

   a. Palliolātella in silvam it ut _____.

      carpere gives us the gerundive _____ -us, -a, -um, "*to be picked*"

   b. Palliolātella in silvam it ad _____.

3. *The stepmother's daughters dress themselves with care, <u>in order to please the king's son</u>.*

   *(in order that they **may please** him)*

   fīlius rēgis, fīliī rēgis, *m. king's son*
   dēlectō, dēlectāre, dēlectāvī, *to please*

   a. Fīliae novercae sibi vestītum magnā cum cūrā induunt ut
   _____ _____.

   dēlectāre gives us the gerundive _____ -us, -a, -um, "to be pleased"

   b. Fīliae novercae sibi vestītum magnā cum cūrā induunt ad
   _____ _____.

II. Gerund vs. Gerundive

The **gerund<u>ive</u>** is an *adject<u>ive</u>*; it is in agreement with a noun.

In the story, the Red Hen asks, "Quis mē ad pānem suāvissimum edendum adiuvābit?", *"Who will help me in eating the very delicious bread?"*

Note that both **suāvissimum** and the gerundive **edendum** are accusative, masculine singular, modifying **pānem** (object of the preposition **ad**).

If the Hen wanted to eat apples (**māla**, *n. pl.*), the gerundive phrase would be written **ad māla suāvissima edenda**.

The **gerund** is a *noun*; like the gerundive, it is formed from the present stem using **-nd-**, but instead of adding the full set of **-us, -a, -um** adjective endings, as the gerundive does, the gerund is a <u>2nd declension neuter noun</u> declined in all cases *except* the nominative:

genitive	**edendī**	*of eating*
dative	**edendō**	*for eating*
accusative	(ad) **edendum**	*for (the purpose of) eating* (following the preposition **ad**)
ablative	**edendō**	*by eating*

As a subject ("<u>Eating</u> is necessary," for example), English uses the –ing noun called the gerund, but Latin uses the verb's <u>present active infinitive</u>: Necesse est edere. (Hence there is no nominative-case gerund in Latin.)

1. Change the following Latin infinitives into gerunds, in the ablative (of means/instrument):

   a. *by working:*   **labōrāre:**   _____
   b. *by helping:*   **adiuvāre:**   _____
   c. *by milling:*   **molere:**   _____
   d. *by cooking:*   **coquere:**   _____
   e. *by arriving:*   **advenīre:**   _____
   (*-io* verbs have the "extra *i*")

2. Translate the following English phrases into Latin using the gerundive. In English, we can have the gerund govern an object, as in "by helping the Little Red Hen" (where she is the direct object of "by helping"). Although Latin sometimes does this (**Gallīnam rūfam adiuvandō**), Latin authors usually preferred to recast the whole structure: what we translate as the direct object in English is put into the same case (here, ablative) as was used by the gerund; and, replacing the gerund, Latin uses the gerundive to modify the noun (it will agree with the noun in gender, number, case): **Gallīnā rūfā adiuvandā**, *"by the Little Red Hen being helped,"* (literally).

   a. *by cooking the bread:*   pāne _____
                                 masc. abl. sing.
   b. *by milling the spelt:*   farre _____
                                 făr, farris, *n.* neut. abl. sing.

Homunculus Condītus Grammar Exercises

I. Adjective, Adverb, *Quam* + Superlative

Given an adjective listing, form the derived adverb, and make the **quam** + superlative (adjective or adverb) structure, which is used to suggest "the highest degree possible" of something.

Then, use these forms to translate the underlined superlative phrase in the English sentence into Latin.

1. The mother bear makes extremely hot porridge.

   hot = calidus, -a, -um

   extremely hot = _____, -a, -um

   hotly, in a hot fashion = calid_____

   a. "The porridge is ready, but it is <u>extremely hot</u>."

      Puls est parāta, sed _____ est.

   b. "Don't eat the porridge <u>that is as hot as it can be</u>!"

      Nōlī pultem quam _____ edere!"

2. Little Red Riding Hood is eager to pick the most beautiful flowers.

    beautiful = pulcher, pulchra, pulchrum

    most beautiful = _____, -a, -um

NB: adjectives ending in **–er** in the masculine nominative singular use the masculine nominative singular form as the base for the superlative that ends in **–rimus**.

    beautifully = pulchr_____

  a. *"I see the <u>most beautiful flowers possible</u> over there; I must leave the path!" says Little Red Riding Hood.*

    "Flōrēs quam _____ illīc videō; dē viā discēdere dēbeō!" ait Palliolātella.

  b. *"I will deceive both the child and the grandmother <u>beautifully</u>!" thinks the Wolf to himself.*

    "Et puellam et aviam _____ dēcipiam!" sibi cōgitat lupus.

3. *The lazy friends of the Little Red Hen are <u>extremely hungry</u> at the end.*

    hungry, empty = iēiūnus, -a, -um

    extremely hungry = _____, -a, -um

    hungrily, in a hungry fashion = iēiūn_____

    "Alas! We have been extremely lazy; now we are <u>as hungry as can be</u>," say the Pig, the Cat, and the Duck.

    Eheu! Pigerrimī fuimus; nunc sumus quam _____, inquiunt porcus et fēlēs et anas.

II. Participles of *Eō, īre, iī, ītum,* "To Go" and Its Compounds

1. Translate the underlined participle in the English sentence into Latin. Remember that the Latin participle must agree in gender, number, and case with the noun it modifies.

   Note the irregular <u>present active participle</u> of **īre: iēns, euntis,** *going.*

   Similarly, **trānseō, trānsīre,** *to go across,* has **trānsiēns, trānseuntis,** *going across.*

   We see that the present active participle is a 3rd declension adjective (note the genitive singular ending in **-is**). Remember to drop the ending **-is** to find the base of the participle (**eunt–**) to which all endings are added.

   a. "Well! I see a charming child, Little Red Riding Hood, <u>going</u> through the woods!" says the Wolf.

   "Eho! Puellam venustam Palliolātellam per silvam _____ videō!" inquit lupus.

   b. The Gingerbread Man, <u>while crossing</u> the river, is tricked by the Fox.

   Homunculus condītus, rīvum _____, ā vulpe dēcipitur.

   c. "I shall speak to Little Red Riding Hood <u>as she is going</u> to her grandmother's house!"

   "Palliolātellae ad aviae casam _____ loquar!"

   d. The Pig, the Cat and the Duck do not remember the Little Red Hen <u>as she is going</u> to the mill.

   Porcus et fēlēs et anas gallīnae rūfae ad molās _____ nōn meminērunt.

   > meminī, meminisse, *to remember* (+ genitive)
   > molae, -ārum, *f. pl. the mill*

2. In the following sentences, translate the underlined English phrase into Latin, using the appropriate form of the gerundive of **eō, īre,** or **trānseō, trānsīre.**

The gerund of **eō, īre** is **eundī** (**eundō, eundum, eundō**), *going,* and the gerundive (in the neuter singular impersonal form) is **eundum.** "He must go" is expressed in Latin impersonally (lit., "it must be gone by him"): **Eī eundum est.** ("He" is in the dative, and "it" is expressed by the neuter ending of the gerundive.)

But some transitive compounds of **īre,** like **trānsīre,** *go across,* and **praeterīre,** *go past,* have the full set of gerundive forms (**trānseundus, -a, -um,** etc.).

a. *"Cinderella <u>must go</u> to the ball!" says the Fairy Godmother.*

   (**īre;** *impersonal*)

   "Cinerellulae ad epulās rēgiās _____ est!" ait Patrōna Faunōrum.

b. *"Little Red Riding Hood <u>will have to go</u> to grandmother's house!" says Mother.*

   "Palliolātellae ad aviae casam _____ erit!" inquit māter.

c. *The Gingerbread Man <u>has to go past</u> various people and animals who want to eat him.*

   Homunculō condītō varia animālia variīque hominēs, quī eum edere volunt, _____ sunt.

   (**praeterīre;** *transitive*)

NB: What gender should be used for "various people and animals," since the animals are neuter and the people are masculine? It is probably best to make the gerundive agree with the people, who are closer in the sentence to the gerundive (so, use the masculine plural nominative form).

TRĒS HIRCĪ ASPERĪ GRAMMAR EXERCISES

I. Active Periphrastic

Form the **future active participle** of the given verb, and then use it as necessary in the "active periphrastic" or **sum + future active participle** construction.

1. vorō, vorāre, vorāvī, *to devour*

    fut. act. ptcpl., _____ "about to devour"

    a. *The wolf is <u>about to devour</u> Little Red Riding Hood! If only a woodcutter would prevent him!*

      Lupus Palliolātellam _____ est. Utinam lignātor quīdam eum prohibeat!

    b. *The Three Bears are <u>about to devour</u> their porridge. However, Baby Bear's bowl is empty.*

      Ursī Trēs pultem _____ sunt. Patella tamen Ursulī est vacua.

2. fugiō, fugere, fūgī, fugitum, *to escape*

    fut. act. ptcpl., _____ "about to escape"

    The Gingerbread Man is <u>on the point of escaping</u>. The wolf, however, catches him and eats him.

    Homunculus condītus _____ est. Vulpēs tamen eum capit et edit.

3. The <u>future active participle</u> can also be used *in any case needed* to modify a noun and express an action that is (or was) about to happen:

    a. *The wolf devoured the Gingerbread Man, <u>who was on the point of escaping</u>.*

      Vulpēs homunculum condītum _____ vorāvit.

b. *The woodcutter chased away the evil wolf, <u>who was about to eat up</u> Little Red Riding Hood and her grandmother.*

Lignātor lupum scelestum Palliolātellam et aviam
_____ reppulit.

II. Comparisons

1. The following comparisons are made using **quam**.

    <u>Translate</u> them into English; then, <u>rewrite</u> the sentences to use the <u>ablative of comparison</u>. (NB: the rewritten sentences will not use **quam**, since comparisons made without **quam** use the *ablative* form of the second member of the comparison.)

    a. Homunculus condītus <u>celerius quam senex</u> currit.

    senex, senis, *m.*

    _____

    _____

    b. Gallīna rūfa est <u>dīligentior quam anas</u>.

    anas, anatis, *m.*

    _____

    _____

    c. Ursus Pater est <u>multō maior quam Ursulus</u>.

    _____

    _____

    d. Fīliae novercae <u>crudēliōrēs quam māter sua sunt</u>.

    māter, mātris, *f.*

    _____

    _____

    e. Ego sum <u>multō minor quam frātrēs meī</u>.

    frāter, frātris, *m.*

    _____

    _____

2. Translate each sentence into Latin twice—once using **quam** to make the comparison and once using the ablative of comparison.

   a. *The Cat and the Pig are lazier than the Little Red Hen.*

   lazy: ignāvus, -a, -um, *adj.* OR piger, pigra, pigrum, *adj.*

   i. _____

   ii. _____

   b. *The oldest brother of the goats is much fiercer than the Gnome.*

   fierce: ferōx, ferōcis, *adj.* OR trux, trucis, *adj.*

   oldest: maximus, -a, -um + abl. of respect <u>nātū</u>

   much: abl. of degree of difference <u>multō</u>

   i. _____

   ii. _____

Trēs Porcellī Grammar Exercises

I. Positive and Negative Purpose Clauses

In the exercises below, fill in the appropriate forms of the missing Latin words. As you complete each indirect command, positive purpose clause, or negative purpose clause, use the context and vocabulary hints to determine which forms you should use.

The present subjunctive is used in clauses that express an *indirect command*; these clauses are governed by a verb like **imperāre** ("to order").

Note that these resemble *purpose clauses*, in that *positive* purposes and commands both are introduced by **ut**, and *negative* purposes and commands are introduced by **ne**. Notice, however, that when the verb **iubere** ("to order") is used, an accusative + infinitive structure is used, instead of **ut/ne** + subjunctive.

1. In the story, the mother pig tells her offspring to leave home and seek out a living:

    Quōdam diē māter eōs iubet discēdere <u>ut victum quaerant</u>.

    How did the piglets report this to each other (indirect command)?

    a. "Mother is ordering <u>us to leave</u>!"

    "Māter _____ iubet _____."

    iubet + accusative + infinitive

    "Māter _____ imperat _____."

    imperat + dative + indirect command

    b. "Mother is ordering <u>us to seek out</u> a living!"

    "Māter _____ iubet victum _____."

    "Māter _____ imperat _____ victum _____."

2. The first piglet buys straw for building a house. In the story, the first piglet expresses his intention as a purpose clause:

   "Salvē, agricola. Vīsne mihi strāmenta vēndere, <u>ut casam mihi construam</u>?"

   Rewrite the purpose clause ("<u>... to build a house</u>") using **ad + the gerundive**:

   Porcellus Prīmus: "Salvē, agricola. Vīsne mihi strāmenta vēndere, ad _____ mihi _____?"
         construō, construere

3. In the story, the second piglet uses a purpose clause to ask the woodcutter to sell him branches:

   Porcellus Alter: "Salvē, lignātor, vīsne mihi rāmōs vendere, <u>ut casam mihi construam</u>?"

   How would this purpose clause change if the narrator explains why the second piglet buys branches? Translate the underlined phrase in the English sentence below into Latin.

   The piglet buys logs, <u>in order to build a house</u>.
         (in order that he may build ...)

   Nārrātor: Porcellus Alter rāmōs emit, _____.

4. The third piglet has seen his two brothers' houses destroyed by the wolf and his brothers eaten. He knows he is in a life-and-death struggle with the wolf!

   The third piglet builds his house with bricks, <u>lest the wolf destroy his house</u> (negative purpose clause):

   Porcellus tertius lateribus casam construit, _____.
         dīruō, dīruere

5. The wolf did destroy the other piglets' houses, unfortunately. We can reconstruct their final pleas to the wolf (negative indirect commands):

Wolf, wolf, I beg you <u>not to devour me</u>!
(... that you not devour me!)

Lupe, lupe, _____ ōrō _____!

ōrō, ōrāre + accusative + indirect command

Lupe, lupe, _____ imperō _____!

imperō, imperāre + dative + indirect command

6. The wolf invents a series of ruses to lure the third piglet out of his brick house; as we see, the piglet is too clever to be caught this way. What does the third piglet do to avoid being eaten (negative purpose clause)?

The third piglet arrives at the garden first, <u>lest the wolf catch him</u>.
Porcellus Tertius ad hortum prior advenit, _____.

The third piglet arrives at the vineyard first, <u>lest he be caught by the wolf</u>.
Porcellus Tertius ad vīneam prior advenit, _____.

    capiō, capere

The third piglet returns home from the ceremony, <u>in order to save himself</u>.
Porcellus Tertius ā sollemnī domum revenit, _____.

    mē servō, sē servāre

7. The desperate finale:

The wolf climbs up <u>in order to enter through the roof</u>.
Lupus ascendit _____ per tēctum _____.

    intrō, intrāre

The piglet puts a pot on the hearth <u>in order to cook the wolf</u>.
Porcellus aēnum in focum pōnit _____.

    coquō, coquere

Nivea Et Septem Nānī
Grammar Exercises

I. Describing the Dwarfs

Other than hearing their names, we don't see much of the Dwarfs in this version of the story; to make up for this, let's describe them here.

<u>Which one is being described</u>? Fill in the names, as appropriate (in the correct cases—to correspond to the case of <u>nānus</u> in each sentence). (See below, for special vocabulary.)

Names: **Stultus, Sternutāns, Laetus, Irācundus, Doctus, Timidus, Dormitāns**

1. Nānus _____ appellātur, quod est ingeniō tardō.

2. Nānum _____ appellant, quod mente callidā est.

3. Omnēs nānum nōmine _____ amant, quī semper rīdet.

4. Omnēs nānum nōmine _____ dērīdent, quod omnia timet.

5. Nānus nōmine _____ gravēdinem semper habet; semper tussit, semper sternuit.

6. Nānus nōmine _____ semper cubitum īre vult; sēmisomnus est.

7. Nānus quem omnēs propter bīlem timent _____ appellātur.

    bīlis, bīlis, *f. gall; anger, displeasure; melancholy*

    callidus, -a, -um, *clever*

    dērīdeō, dērīdēre, dērīsī, dērīsus, *to mock, laugh at*

    gravēdō, gravēdinis, *f. cold*

    ingenium, -ī, *n. talent, cleverness*

    mens, mentis, *f. mind*

    sternuō, sternuere, sternuī, *to sneeze*

    tardus, -a, -um, *slow (of comprehension)*

    tussiō, tussīre, *to cough*

II. Ablative Absolute Used to Express What One Wishes For

The wicked queen hopes that she can kill Snow White and regain the title of most beautiful in the land. She first tries to have the woodcutter abandon the child in the forest:

> Niveā in silvā relictā, pulcherrima omnium quae in rēgnō sunt ego erō!
>
> *When Snow White has been abandoned in the forest, I will be the most beautiful . . . !*

It's as if she were saying, "**If** Nivea is abandoned . . . " or "**Once** Nivea has been abandoned"; the ablative absolute functions here as **a very positive form of a condition** (= *if-clause*).

In the exercises below, complete the Latin sentence by using the ablative absolute to express the underlined portion of the English sentence. Refer to the vocabulary hints below each exercise if needed.

1. When the queen discovers that Snow White is still alive, she thinks of a new way to kill her:

    When the apple has been eaten, I will be the most beautiful again!

    _____, pulcherrima omnium rūrsus erō!

    When the girl has been killed, I will be the most beautiful again!

    _____, pulcherrima omnium rūrsus erō!

    When the poison has been given, I will be the most beautiful again!

    _____, pulcherrima omnium rūrsus erō!

    dō, dare, dedī, datus, *to give*
    edō, edere, ēdī, ēsus, *to eat*
    interficiō, interficere, interfēcī, interfectus, *to kill*
    mālum, -ī, *n. apple*
    venēnum, -ī, *n. poison*

2. When the prince comes, he hopes that he'll be able to wake the beautiful girl in the time-honored way of fairy tales:

<u>When the kiss has been given,</u> the girl will wake up!

_____ , puella surget!

    ōsculum, -ī, *n. kiss*

3. When Snow White sees the cottage belonging to the Dwarfs, she imagines how nice it would look if cleaned up a little:

<u>When the little house has been cleaned,</u>

_____

<u>when the dishes have been washed,</u>

_____

<u>when the beds have been made,</u>

_____

how happy I will be!

quam laeta erō!

    casa, -ae, *f. little house*
    pūrgō, pūrgāre, pūrgāvī, pūrgātus, *to clean*
    patella, -ae, *f. dish*
    lavō, lavāre, lāvī, lautus/lavātus, *to wash*
    lectus, -ī, *m. bed*
    compōnō, compōnere, composuī, compositus,
       to put together, arrange

Fistulātor Versicolor Hamelīnus Grammar Exercises

I. *Opus Est*

For each of the following sentences, how else could the speaker express the statement? Given one **opus est** construction, change the wording as necessary to make the other two. Use the vocabulary aids and instructions to help you.

1. Māter porcellī (mother of the piglets): *Go on, piglets, it is necessary to leave home.*

    Agite, porcellī, opus est domō <u>proficīscī</u>.

    opus est + infinitive

    proficīscor, proficīscī, profectus sum,
      to set out, depart, leave

    a. <u>Use opus **est** + **ut** + subjunctive</u>:

       Agite, porcellī, opus est ut domō _____.

       ("... that you all leave home," i.e., 2nd person plural present subjunctive)

    b. <u>Use **opus est** + ablative</u>:

       profectiō, profectiōnis, *f. departure*

       vester, vestra, vestrum, *belonging to you (pl.)*

       Agite, porcellī, opus est _____.

       ("... there is need of your departure")

2. Homunculus Condītus: *I must get across the river.*

    Opus est mihi ut rīvum transeam.

    trānseō, trānsīre, trānsiī, trānsitus, *to go across*

    trānsitus, -ūs, *m. crossing*

    a. <u>Use **opus est** + infinitive</u>:

       Opus est _____.

    b. <u>Use **opus est** + ablative</u>:

       Opus est _____.

3. Homunculus Condītus: *I must sit on the fox's muzzle.*

   Opus est sessiōne in rostrō vulpis.

   sedeō, sedēre, sēdī, *to sit*

   sessiō, sessiōnis, *f. sitting*

   a. Use **opus est** + **ut** + subjunctive:

   Opus est _____.

   b. Use **opus est** + infinitive:

   Opus est _____.

II. Future More Vivid, Future Less Vivid

Match the statements with the characters (see **choices,** *below*). Does the character sound **positive (FMV)** or more **doubtful (FLV)** about what will happen? Write your answers in the blanks provided.

The **future indicative** expresses a positive view of what will happen: "It will rain tomorrow." It's as "factual" (the mood is indicative, after all) as something that hasn't yet happened can be. By contrast, one use of the **present subjunctive** is to represent a *hypothetical* or merely possible statement about the future: "It may rain tomorrow."

In Latin, there are two types of conditional statements ("if, then") that look to the future. One, called Future More Vivid (FMV), uses future indicative in both clauses: "If it will rain, we will stay home." The speaker sounds very positive and certain about what will happen.* The other type, called Future Less Vivid (FLV), uses the present subjunctive in both clauses: "If it should rain, we would stay home." The mood of the speaker seems doubtful or hesitant.

*Note that, given Latin's logical view of tense relationships, the FMV "positive" type is likely to use the **future perfect indicative** in the "if"-clause: "If it will have rained (which must happen *first*), we will stay home tomorrow."

1. Sī septem nānī nōbīscum habitent, vītam beātam agāmus.

   Character: _____ Type of condition: _____

2. Avia gaudēbit sī flōrēs pulchrōs eī afferam.

   Character: _____ Type of condition: _____

3. Fīlius rēgis fīliārum alteram <u>ēliget</u>, sī modo soleam vitream <u>induerit</u>.
   Character: _____ Type of condition: _____

4. Sī casam porcellī <u>īnflābō</u>, casa <u>dīruētur</u>, porcellus ā mē <u>vorābitur</u>.
   Character: _____ Type of condition: _____

5. Sī casam lateribus <u>construam</u>, lupus eam īnflandō dīruere nōn <u>possit</u>.
   Character: _____ Type of condition: _____

6. Rēgīna nihil <u>cognōscet</u>, sī puellulam in hāc casā <u>relīquerō</u>.
   Character: _____ Type of condition: _____

7. Sī puellae ōsculum <u>dederō</u>, statim <u>surget</u>.
   Character: _____ Type of condition: _____

8. Fīlia tua <u>moriētur</u>, sī fūsum digitō <u>tanget</u>.
   Character: _____ Type of condition: _____

9. Sī Magister Hamelīnus mihi praemium nōn <u>solvat</u>, līberī numquam anteā <u>videantur</u>.
   Character: _____ Type of condition: _____

10. Sī septem nānī nōbīscum <u>habitābunt</u>, vītam quam beātissimam <u>agēmus</u>.
    Character: _____ Type of condition: _____

Choices:
a. Fīlius rēgis (from *Puella Pulchra Quae Dormiēbat*)
b. Fīlius rēgis (from *Nivea et Septem Nānī*)
c. Fistulātor
d. Lignātor (from *Nivea et Septem Nānī*)
e. Lupus (from *Trēs Porcellī*)
f. Nivea
g. Noverca
h. Nympha quarta (from *Puella Pulchra Quae Dormiēbat*)
i. Palliolātella
j. Porcellus tertius

Puella Pulchra Quae Dormiēbat Grammar Exercises

I. Gift-Giving Expressions

Practice changing from one gift-giving expression to another by translating the following sentences from English to Latin. Use the vocabulary aids to help you determine what words and constructions to use.

1. *Palliolātella:*

    I will give food and medicines to grandmother.

    Aviae cibum et medicāmina dabō.

    a. *I will present grandmother with food and medicines.*

    dōnāre + accusative of person, ablative of thing(s) given

    _____

    b. *I will send food and medicines to grandmother for a present.*

    mittere + accusative of thing(s), dative for recipient, + dative of purpose

    _____

2. *Anus:*

    I will present my household with a gingerbread man.

    Familiam meam homunculō condītō dōnābō.

    a. *I will give my household a gingerbread man.*

    dare + accusative of thing, dative for recipient

    _____

    b. *I will send a gingerbread man to my household as a gift.*

    mittere + accusative of thing, dative for recipient, + dative of purpose

    _____

3. *Auricoma:*

I will send money as a present to the Bears, to pay for the broken chair.

Ursīs pecūniam mūnerī mittō, ut sella frācta luātur.

luō, luere, luī, *to expiate; pay for*

a. *I should present the Bears with money, to pay for the broken chair.*

dōnāre (in the present subjunctive) + accusative of person, ablative of thing

---

b. *If I will give money to the Bears as a gift, the broken chair will be paid for!*

dare + accusative + dative (indirect object) + dative (of purpose), expressed as . . . FMV, or FLV? Is Goldilocks using the present subjunctive, or the future indicative? Review the difference between the two types of conditional sentences in the exercise from **Fistulātor Versicolor Hamelīnus,** pages 106–107.

Latin to English Glossary

Abbreviations

abl. = ablative
acc. = accusative
adj. = adjective
adv. = adverb
compar. = comparative
conj. = conjunction
dat. = dative
dimin. = diminutive
distrib. = distributive
f. = feminine
gen. = genitive
impers. = impersonal
indecl. = indeclinable
infin. = infinitive

interj. = interjection
interrog. = interrogative
lit. = literally
m. = masculine
n. = neuter
nom. = nominative
pers. = person
pl. = plural
prn. = pronoun
reflex. = reflexive
sing. = singular
superl. = superlative
voc. = vocative

– A –

ā, + *abl.*, from
abeō, abīre, abiī to go away
absum, abesse, afuī to be away, be absent
accēdō, accēdere, accessī to approach
accidit, accidere, accidit (*impers.*) to happen
accipiō, accipere, accēpī, acceptus to receive, take
ācer, ācris, ācre sharp
acerbus, -a, -um bitter, harsh
ad, + *acc.*, to
adfor, adfārī, adfātus est to speak to, address
adhūc, *adv.* still
adiuvō, adiuvāre, adiūvī, adiūtus to help
admīror, admīrārī, admīrātus sum to marvel at
adsum, adesse, adfuī to be present
adulēscēns, adulēscentis, *m./f.* young person
adveniō, advenīre, advēnī to reach, arrive (at)
aedēs, aedium, *f. pl.* house
aedificium, -ī, *n.* building
aeger, aegra, aegrum sick
aegrōtō, aegrōtāre, aegrōtāvī to be sick
aēnum, -ī, *n.* bronze vessel, cauldron
affectus, -a, -um affected (by) (+ *abl.*)
afferō, afferre, attulī, allātus to bring (toward), bring along
afflō, afflare, afflāvī, afflātus to blow (on)
age, *interj.* come on!
ager, agrī, *m.* field
agō, agere, ēgī, āctus to do
  fābulam agere to put on a play
agricola, -ae, *m.* farmer
aliēnus, -a, -um foreign, strange
alimentum, -ī, *n.* food
aliōquī, *adv.* in another way, all the same
aliquis, aliquid someone, something
alter, altera, alterum the other, a second, one (of two)
altus, -a, -um high, deep
amābō, amābō tē please (*lit.,* I will love, I will love you)
amārus, -a, -um bitter
ambō, ambae, ambō both
ambulō, ambulāre, ambulāvī to walk
amīcus, -a, -um friendly
  amīca, -ae, *f.* friend
  amīcus, -ī, *m.* friend
amō, amāre, amāvī, amātus to love
anas, anatis, *f.* duck
angustus, -a, -um narrow
annus, -ī, *m.* year
  sex annōs nāta six years old
ante, + *acc.*, before
anus, -ūs, *f.* old woman
aperiō, aperīre, aperuī, apertus to open
apertē, *adv.* openly
appāreō, appārēre, appāruī to appear, be visible
appellō, appellāre, appellāvī, appellātus to call, name
appropinquō, appropinquāre, appropinquāvī to approach (+ *dat.* or + **ad** + *acc.*)
aptē, *adv.* fittingly, appropriately

apud, + *acc.*, at the house of
aqua, -ae, *f.* water
arbor, arboris, *f.* tree
ascendō, ascendere, ascendī to climb
asper, aspera, asperum rough, harsh
at, *conj.* but
atque, *conj.* and, and also
atrōx, atrōcis terrible, fierce, savage
audiō, audīre, audīvī, audītus to hear
augescō, augescere, auxī to increase, grow
aureus, -a, -um golden
auris, auris, *f.* ear
Auricoma, -ae, *f.* Goldilocks (*from* **aurum, -ī,** *n.* gold *and* **coma, -ae,** *f.* hair)
auxilium, -ī, *n.* help
avia, -ae, *f.* grandmother
avis, avis, *f.* bird

– B –
beātus, -a, -um happy, fortunate, blessed
bellus, -a, -um pretty, charming, nice
bene, *adv.* well
benevolus, -a, -um kind, friendly
bonus, -a, -um good
brevis, -e short, brief

– C –
cadō, cadere, cecidī to fall
calamitās, calamitātis, *f.* disaster
calidus, -a, -um hot
canis, canis, *m./f.* dog
cantō, cantāre, cantāvī, cantātus to sing; to play music on (+ *abl.*)
cantus, -ūs, *m.* song, music
capillus, -ī, *m.* hair
capiō, capere, cēpī, captus to take, seize
caput, capitis, *n.* head
careō, carēre, caruī to lack (+ *abl.*)
carmen, carminis, *n.* song
carpō, carpere, carpsī, carptus to pick, pluck
cārus, -a, -um dear, beloved
casa, -ae, *f.* hut, cottage
cauda, -ae, *f.* tail
caveō, cavēre, cāvī, cautus to beware of, watch out for
celebrō, celebrāre, celebrāvī, celebrātus to observe, celebrate (a day)
celer, celeris, celere quick
celeriter, *adv.* quickly
cēlō, cēlāre, cēlāvī, cēlātus to hide
sē cēlāre to hide oneself
cēna, -ae, *f.* dinner
cēnō, cēnāre, cēnāvī to dine, have dinner
centum, *indecl. adj.* one hundred
cibus, -ī, *m.* food
Cinerellula, -ae, *f.* Cinderella (*from* **cinis, cineris,** *m.* ash + **-ula,** *femin. dimin. suffix*)
circum, + *acc.*, around
circumdō, circumdāre, circumdedī, circumdatus to surround, put around
clāmō, clāmāre, clāmāvī to shout, exclaim

clāmor, clāmōris, *m.* a shout
colligō, colligere, collēgī, collectus to gather, pick up
commodus, -a, -um convenient, suitable, comfortable
compleō, complēre, complēvī, complētus to fill
compōnō, compōnere, composuī, compositus to put together, arrange
concēdō, concēdere, concessī to give way, grant, permit
condītus, -a, -um seasoned, flavored
cōnfestim, *adv.* immediately
cōnficiō, cōnficere, cōnfēcī, cōnfectus to finish, make, complete
cōnsentiō, cōnsentīre, cōnsēnsī to agree
cōnstituō, cōnstituere, cōnstituī, cōnstitūtus to decide
cōnstruō, cōnstruere, cōnstruxī, cōnstructus to build
cōnsūmō, cōnsūmere, cōnsūmpsī, cōnsūmptus to eat up
conveniō, convenīre, convēnī to come together, meet
coquō, coquere, coxī, coctus to cook
cōram, + *abl.,* in the presence of
corripiō, corripere, corripuī, correptus to seize
cotīdiē, *adv.* every day, daily
crās, *adv.* tomorrow
crēdō, crēdere, crēdidī, crēditus to believe (+ *dat.*)
crescō, crescere, crēvī, crētus to increase, grow
crīnēs, crīnium, *m. pl.* hair
cruciō, cruciāre, cruciāvī, cruciātus to torture
crūdēlis, -e cruel, savage
crustulum, -ī, *n.* small cake, cookie
cubiculum, -ī, *n.* bedroom
cubitum īre to go to bed (*acc. supine of* **cubāre,** to lie down, + *conjugated forms of* **īre,** to go)
cucurbita, -ae, *f.* gourd
culīna, -ae, *f.* kitchen
cum, *conj.* when
cum, + *abl.,* with
cūr, *adv.* why?
cūrō, cūrāre, cūrāvī, cūrātus to look after, care for
currō, currere, cucurrī to run

— D —

dē, + *abl.,* about, concerning, down from
dēbeō, dēbēre, dēbuī, dēbitus to owe; ought to (+ *infin.*)
decimus, -a, -um tenth
dēcipiō, dēcipere, dēcepī, dēceptus to deceive
dēfessus, -a, -um tired
deī, -ōrum, *m. pl.* the gods
deinde, *adv.* next, then
dēleō, dēlēre, dēlēvī, dēlētus to destroy
dēnārius, -ī, *m.* denarius (silver coin)
dēns, dentis, *m.* tooth
dēpellō, dēpellere, dēpulī, dēpulsus to push down
dērīdeō, dērīdēre, dērīsī to laugh at, mock

dēsīderō, dēsīderāre, dēsīderāvī, dēsīderātus to long for
dīcō, dīcere, dīxī, dictus to say
diēs, diēī, *m.* day
digitus, -ī, *m.* finger
dīruō, dīruere, dīruī, dīrutus to destroy
discēdō, discēdere, discessī to leave
dissentiō, dissentīre, dissēnsī to disagree
dissimilis, -e different from (+ *dat.*)
dissolvō, dissolvere, dissoluī, dissolūtus to solve (a problem)
dō, dare, dedī, datus to give
doceō, docēre, docuī, doctus to teach
    doctus, -a, -um learned, wise, taught
dolābra, -ae, *f.* ax
dolor, dolōris, *m.* grief, sadness
dolus, -ī, *m.* trick
domesticus, -a, -um belonging to the house
    rēs domestica the housework
domina, -ae, *f.* lady (of the house); *as voc.,* madam
dominus, -ī, *m.* master; *as voc.,* sir
domus, -ūs, *f.* house
dōnec, *conj.* until (+ *subjunctive*)
dōnō, dōnāre, dōnāvī, dōnātus to give; to present (someone) with (something)
dōnum, -ī, *n.* gift
dormiō, dormīre, dormīvī to sleep
dormītō, dormītāre, dormītāvī to be drowsy
duo, duae, duo two

dūcō, dūcere, dūxī, ductus to lead
    in mātrimōnium dūcere to take (a bride) in marriage
dulcis, -e sweet
dum, *conj.* while
dumētum, -ī, *n.* a thicket, clump of bushes
duodeciēns, *adv.* twelve times
dūrus, -a, -um hard

– E –

ē, ex, + *abl.,* from, out of
ecce, *interj.* look!
edō, edere, ēdī, ēsus to eat
effugiō, effugere, effūgī to escape from
ego, *1st pers. sing. prn. (nom.)* I
ēgredior, ēgredī, ēgressus sum to leave, go out from
ēheu, *interj.* oh, no!
eho, *interj.* hey!
ēligō, ēligere, ēlēgī, ēlectus to choose
emō, emere, ēmī, ēmptus to buy
enim, *conj.* indeed, for
eō, *adv.* there, to that place
eō, īre, iī to go
epulae, -ārum, *f. pl.* banquet, feast
ergō, *conj.* therefore, and so
et, *conj.* and
etiam, *adv.* even
euge, *interj.* hooray!
eugepae, *interj.* hooray!
ēvānēscō, ēvānēscere, ēvānuī to vanish
evax, *interj.* hurrah! (expressing triumph)

excēdō, excēdere, excessī to go out from
excipiō, excipere, excēpī, exceptus to catch
excitō, excitāre, excitāvī, excitātus to rouse, awaken (someone)
exclāmō, exclāmāre, exclāmāvī to shout (out)
exeō, exīre, exiī to go out
exitus, -ūs, *m.* end, conclusion
exspectō, exspectāre, exspectāvī, exspectātus to wait for
extrahō, extrahere, extraxī, extractus to drag out
extrēmus, -a, -um furthest; the edge of

– F –

fābula, -ae, *f.* story, tale; play
　fābulam agere to put on a story, act a play
faciō, facere, fēcī, factus to do, make
　iter facere to travel, make a journey
familia, -ae, *f.* household, family
fār, farris, *n.* spelt; husked wheat
farīna, -ae, *f.* flour
fatuus, -a, -um fool(ish)
faunus, -ī, *m.* gnome, troll
faunī, -ōrum, *m. pl.* deities of the countryside; fairies, sprites
fēlēs, fēlis, *f.* cat
fēmina, -ae, *f.* woman
fera, -ae, *f.* wild beast
ferō, ferre, tulī, lātus to bring, carry
ferveō, fervēre, ferbuī to be boiling hot
fidēs, fideī, *f.* faith, trust

fīlia, -ae, *f.* daughter
fīlius, -ī, *m.* son
fīliōla, -ae, *f.* little daughter
fingō, fingere, finxī, fictus to devise, contrive, fashion
fīnis, fīnis, *m.* end, finish, limit
　fīnēs, fīnium, *m. pl.* territories, boundaries, land
fīō, fierī, factus sum to happen, become, be made
fistula, -ae, *f.* pipe, fife
fistulātor, fistulātōris, *m.* piper
flātus, -ūs, *m.* blast, blowing
flētus, -ūs, *m.* weeping
flō, flāre, flāvī, flātus to blow
flōs, flōris, *m.* flower
fluō, fluere, fluxī to flow
flūvius, -ī, *m.* river
focus, -ī, *m.* hearth, fireplace
foedus, -a, -um foul, ugly, hideous
forma, -ae, *f.* beauty
formōsus, -a, -um beautiful
forsitan, *adv.* perhaps
fortūnātus, -a, -um lucky, fortunate
frāctus, -a, -um broken
frāter, frātris, *m.* brother
frīgidus, -a, -um cold
furnus, -ī, *m.* oven
fūsus, -ī, *m.* spindle (on a spinning wheel)

– G –

gallīna, -ae, *f.* hen
gemma, -ae, *f.* jewel
Germānī, -ōrum, *m. pl.* the Germans
gerō, gerere, gessī, gestus to wear
glōriōsus, -a, -um boastful, haughty, proud

grātia, -ae, *f.* kindness, goodwill
grātiās agere (+ *dat.*), to thank someone
graviter, *adv.* seriously, heavily
gustō, gustāre, gustāvī, gustātus to taste

– H –
habeō, habēre, habuī, habitus to have
habitō, habitāre, habitāvī, habitātus to dwell, inhabit
habitus, -ūs, *m.* suit of clothing
Hamelīnum, -ī, *n.* the town of Hamelin
herba, -ae, *f.* grass
heu, *interj.* oh, no!
hic, haec, hoc this; *pl.* these
hīc, *adv.* here, in this place
hircus, -ī, *m.* billy goat
hodiē, *adv.* today
homō, hominis, *m.* person, human being
homunculus, -ī, *m.* little man
hōra, -ae, *f.* hour
horribilis, -e terrible, awful
hortus, -ī, *m.* garden
hospes, hospitis, *m./f.* guest
hūc, *adv.* to this place, to here
humilis, -e humble, lowly

– I –
iaceō, iacēre, iacuī to lie
iam, *adv.* now, already
iānua, -ae, *f.* door
   iānuam pulsāre to knock on the door
ibi, *adv.* there

īdem, eadem, idem the same
idōneus, -a, -um suitable
iēiūnus, -a, -um hungry, empty
ientāculum, -ī, *n.* breakfast
igitur, *conj.* therefore, in that case
ille, illa, illud that; *pl.* those (remote from speaker)
illīc, *adv.* there, in that place
imperō, imperāre, imperāvī, imperātus to order
impius, -a, -um wicked, immoral
impossibilis, -e not possible
imprīmīs, *adv.* especially
in, + *abl.*, in, on
   + *acc.*, into, onto
incipiō, incipere, incēpī, inceptus to begin
incolumis, -e safe and sound, unhurt
inde, *adv.* from there; from then on (in time)
induō, induere, induī, indūtus to put on (clothing)
   indūtus, -a, -um dressed in (+ *abl.*)
ineō, inīre, iniī to go into
īnfāns, īnfantis, *m./f.* baby, little child
īnferō, īnferre, intulī, illātus to bring into
inficiō, inficere, infēcī, infectus to imbue, stain with (+ *abl.*)
īnflō, īnflāre, īnflāvī, īnflātus to blow into
ingēns, ingentis huge
ingredior, ingredī, ingressus sum to enter
iniciō, inicere, iniēcī, iniectus to throw (something) upon

inquit he/she says (used with direct quotations)
īnspiciō, īnspicere, īnspexī, īnspectus to examine
intellegō, intellegere, intellexī, intellectus to understand
intervallum, -ī, *n.* space between, gap
intrō, intrāre, intrāvī to enter
inveniō, invenīre, invēnī, inventus to find, come upon
invītō, invītāre, invītāvī, invītātus to invite
iō, *interj.* (a cry of joy)
ipse, ipsa, ipsum, *intensifying prn./ adj.* himself, herself, itself
  eō ipsō tempore at that very moment
īrācundus, -a, -um bad-tempered, grouchy
īrātus, -a, -um angry
is, ea, id, *3rd pers. prn.* he, she, it
iste, ista, istud that (of yours), that (awful)
ita, *adv.* thus, in this way
  ita vērō, *adv.* yes, yes indeed
itaque, *adv.* accordingly, and so
iter, itineris, *n.* journey, trip, route
  iter facere to travel, make a journey
iterum, *adv.* again
iubeō, iubēre, iussī, iussus to order
iūcundus, -a, -um pleasant, delightful

– L –
labellum, -ī, *n.* lip
lābor, lābī, lāpsus sum to slip; (of time) to pass by
labor, labōris, *m.* work
labōrō, labōrāre, labōrāvī to work
lacrimō, lacrimāre, lacrimāvī to cry
laetus, -a, -um happy
lalla (sound of singing) la, la, la
lāna, -ae, *f.* wool
  lānam trahere to spin wool
laqueus, -ī, *m.* lasso
later, lateris, *m.* brick, tile
latrīna, -ae, *f.* bathroom
lavō, lavāre, lāvī, lautus/lavātus to wash
lectus, -ī, *m.* bed
libenter, *adv.* gladly, willingly
līberō, līberāre, līberāvī, līberātus to free (from, + *abl.*)
līberī, -ōrum, *m. pl.* children
libet, libēre, libuit it is pleasing (+ *infin.*)
licet, licēre, licuit it is allowed (+ *infin.*)
lignātor, lignātōris, *m.* woodcutter
locus, -ī, *m.* place
loquor, loquī, locūtus sum to speak, say
lūdō, lūdere, lūsī, lūsus to play
lūdibrium, -ī, *n.* toy; laughingstock
lupus, -ī, *m.* wolf
lustricus, -a, -um (+ **diēs,** day) the day a newborn child was named
lūx, lūcis, *f.* light
  prīmā lūce (*abl. of time*) at dawn, at first light

– M –
madidus, -a, -um wet, dripping
magicus, -a, -um having to do with magic, magical

magister, magistrī, *m.* mayor (of a town)
magnopere, *adv.* greatly
magnus, -a, -um big, large, great
maior, maius bigger (*compar. of* **magnus**)
mālum, -ī, *n.* apple
māne, *adv.* early, in the morning
maneō, manēre, mānsī to stay
margarīta, -ae, *f.* pearl
māter, mātris, *f.* mother
mātrimōnium, -ī, *n.* marriage
　in mātrimōnium dūcere to take (a bride) in marriage
maximus, -a, -um biggest, greatest (*superl. of* **magnus**)
mē, *1st pers. sing. prn.* (*abl./acc.; nom. is* **ego**) me
medicāmen, medicāminis, *n.* medicine
mediocris, -e middle-sized, medium
medius, -a, -um mid; the middle of
　media nox midnight
melior, melius better (*compar. of* **bonus**)
meminī, meminisse to remember
mendācium, -ī, *n.* lie, falsehood
mēnsa, -ae, *f.* table
mēnsis, mēnsis, *m.* month
meritus, -a, -um deserved, earned
messis, messis, *f.* harvest, reaping
meus, -a, -um my, mine
mihi, *1st pers. sing. prn.* (*dat.; nom. is* **ego**) to/for me
mille, *indecl. adj.* a thousand
minimē, *adv.* in the least, no, not at all

minimus, -a, -um smallest (*superl. of* **parvus**)
　minima nātū the youngest (*lit.,* smallest in birth)
miser, misera, miserum wretched, unhappy, miserable
　Ō mē miseram! o poor me! (*exclamatory acc.*)
miserābilis, -e pitiable, unfortunate
mittō, mittere, mīsī, missus to send
modo, *adv.* only, just
molō, molere, moluī, molitus to grind grain into flour
mollis, -e soft
momentum, -ī, *n.* importance
　maximī momentī (*gen. of value*) of greatest importance
monīle, monīlis, *n.* necklace
mōns, montis, *m.* mountain
morbus, -ī, *m.* disease
morior, morī, mortuus sum to die
mors, mortis, *f.* death
mortuus, -a, -um dead
mox, *adv.* soon
multus, -a, -um much
　multō (*abl. of degree of difference*) by much
mūnus, mūneris, *n.* gift
mūs, mūris, *m.* rodent, mouse, rat
mūsica, -ae, *f.* music

– N –
nam, *conj.* for
nānus, -ī, *m.* dwarf
nārrātor, nārrātōris, *m.* narrator
nārrō, nārrāre, nārrāvī, nārrātus to tell, relate

nātū, *abl. sing.,* by birth (used to indicate age)
   minima nātū the youngest (in birth)
nātus, -a, -um (*participle of* **nāscī**) born; + *acc. of time,* old
   sex annōs nāta six years old (*lit.,* born/alive for six years)
-ne, *interrog. particle* (indicates that a yes/no question is being asked)
nē, *conj.* lest, that not (+ *subjunctive*)
nec (*and* **neque**), *conj.* and not
necō, necāre, necāvī, necātus to kill
necesse, *indecl. adj. n.* necessary, unavoidable
nēmō, nēminis, *m./f.* no one
neque (*and* **nec**), *conj.* and not
   neque . . . neque neither . . . nor
nequeō, nequīre, nequīvī to be unable (+ *infin.*)
niger, nigra, nigrum black
nīmīrum, *adv.* doubtless, certainly
nimium, *adv.* too much, very much
nisi, *conj.* if not, unless
niveus, -a, -um snowy white
nōbīs, *1st pers. pl. prn.* (*dat./abl.; nom. is* **nōs**) for us, with us
nōlī (+ *infin., negative command*) Don't . . . !
nōlō, nōlle, nōluī to not want, refuse, be unwilling
nōmen, nōminis, *n.* name
nōn, *adv.* not
nōndum, *adv.* not yet
nōs, *1st pers. pl. prn.* we, us
noscō, noscere, nōvī, nōtus to become acquainted with
   nōtus, -a, -um known, familiar
nōvī (perfect with present meaning) know
noster, nostra, nostrum our
novem, *indecl. adj.* nine
noverca, -ae, *f.* stepmother
novus, -a, -um new
nox, noctis, *f.* night
nūbō, nūbere, nupsī, nupta (of a woman) to marry, to be given in marriage to (+ *dat.*)
nūgae, -ārum, *f. pl.* nonsense, idle talk, trifles
nūllus, -a, -um not any, none
num, *interrog.* (introduces a question that expects the answer "no")
numquam, *adv.* never
nunc, *adv.* now
nūntiō, nūntiāre, nūntiāvī, nūntiātus to announce, report
nūntius, -ī, *m.* messenger
nūptiae, -ārum, *f. pl.* wedding
nympha, -ae, *f.* nymph, female spirit (fairy)

– O –

ō, *interj.* oh (+ *voc.*)
obdormiō, obdormīre, obdormīvī to fall asleep
oblīviscor, oblīviscī, oblītus sum to forget (+ *gen.*)
oculus, -ī, *m.* eye
odor, odōris, *m.* smell, scent, fragrance
oleō, olēre, oluī to smell of, be redolent of
olfaciō, olfacere, olfēcī, olfactus to scent, sniff
ōlim, *adv.* once (upon a time)

omnis, -e each, every; *pl.*, all
opera, -ae, *f.* effort, trouble
oportet, oportēre, oportuit it is proper, right (+ *infin.*)
oppidānus, -ī, *m.* townsman
oppidum, -ī, *n.* town
optimē, *adv.* excellently, very well
optimus, -a, -um excellent (*superl. of* **bonus**)
opus, operis, *n.* work, task, activity, effort
   opus est there is need of, it's necessary
ōsculor, ōsculārī, ōsculātus sum to kiss
ōsculum, -ī, *n.* kiss

– P –

palla, -ae, *f.* cloak (worn by women)
Palliolātella, -ae, *f.* Little Red Riding Hood (formed on the model of **palliolātus,** used by Suetonius [*Claudius* 2.2])
palliolum, -ī, *n.* a small cloak
pānis, pānis, *m.* bread
parēns, parentis, *m./f.* parent
pārens, pārentis (*participle of* **pārēre**), obedient
pāreō, pārēre, pāruī to obey (+ *dat.*)
pariēs, parietis, *m.* wall
pariō, parere, peperī, partus to give birth to
parō, parāre, parāvī, parātus to prepare
   sē parāre to get (oneself) ready
pars, partis, *f.* part
parvulus, -a, -um small, very small, tiny (*dimin. of* **parvus**)

parvus, -a, -um small
patella, -ae, *f.* small dish or plate
pater, patris, *m.* father
patrōna, -ae, *f.* patroness, protectress; godmother
pavīmentum, -ī, *n.* paved flooring
pecūnia, -ae, *f.* money
per, + *acc.*, through
pereō, perīre, periī to die
perfidus, -a, -um treacherous, false, faithless
perīculōsus, -a, -um dangerous
perpetuus, -a, -um lasting, eternal
   in perpetuum forever, in perpetuity
persolvō, persolvere, persolvī, persolūtus to pay in full; to resolve
perterritus, -a, -um frightened, terrified
perveniō, pervenīre, pervēnī to arrive at
pēs, pedis, *m.* foot; paw
petō, petere, petīvī, petītus to seek, look for, head for
piger, pigra, pigrum lazy, slothful, idle
pīlentum, -ī, *n.* luxurious carriage (used by women)
piscātor, piscātōris, *m.* fisherman
piscis, piscis, *m.* fish
placeō, placēre, placuī, placitus to be pleasing, acceptable to (+ *dat.*)
plānē, *adv.* clearly
plēnus, -a, -um full (of) (+ *gen.*)
plūrēs, -a more, very many (*compar. of* **multī**)
plūrimī, -ae, -a very many, most (*superl. of* **multī**)

pōmum, -ī, *n.* fruit
pōnō, pōnere, posuī, positus to put, place
pōns, pontis, *m.* bridge
populus, -ī, *m.* population, people
porcellus, -ī, *m.* piglet (*dimin. of* **porcus**)
porcus, -ī, *m.* pig
portō, portāre, portāvī, portātus to carry
possibilis, possibile possible
possum, posse, potuī to be able
post, + *acc.,* after, behind
post, *adv.* later
posteā, *adv.* later on, afterward
posterus, -a, -um later, next, following
   posterō diē (*abl. of time*) on the next day
posthāc, *adv.* thereafter, from then on
postrēmō, *adv.* finally, last of all, at last
postulō, postulāre, postulāvī, postulātus to demand
potens, potentis (*participle of* **possum**) powerful, capable
praeclārē, *adv.* clearly; very well, excellently
praeclārus, -a, -um famous, distinguished, well-known
praemium, -ī, *n.* reward
praepōnō, praepōnere, praeposuī, praepositus to prefer, value more, put (*acc.*) before (*dat.*)
praetereō, praeterīre, praeteriī to go by, pass
pretiōsus, -a, -um valuable, precious
pretium, -ī, *n.* price, value

prīmum, *adv.* first
prīmus, -a, -um first, foremost
   prīmā lūce (*abl. of time*) at first light, at dawn
prior, prius before, earlier, preceding
probō, probāre, probāvī, probātus to try, test, prove
procul, *adv.* in the distance, far off
proficīscor, proficīscī, profectus sum to set out, depart
prope, + *acc.,* near, next to
propius, *adv.* closer, nearer
prōpōnō, prōpōnere, prōposuī, prōpositus to set forth, propose
prōscrībō, prōscrībere, prōscrīpsī, prōscrīptus to publish someone's name as an outlaw
prūdēns, prūdentis wise, sensible
puella, -ae, *f.* girl
puellula, -ae, *f.* little girl (*dimin. of* **puella**)
puer, puerī, *m.* boy
pulcher, pulchra, pulchrum beautiful, handsome
pūlex, pūlicis, *m.* flea
puls, pultis, *f.* porridge
pulsō, pulsāre, pulsāvī, pulsātus to strike, beat
   iānuam pulsāre to knock on the door
pūrgō, pūrgāre, pūrgāvī, pūrgātus to clean

– Q –

quaerō, quaerere, quaesīvī, quaesītus to look for, search for
quālis, -e what sort of, what type of

quam, *adv.* How … ! (+ *adj.*)
   quam, + *superl.,* as ~ as possible;
   quam celerrimē, *adv.* as fast as possible
quārtus, -a, -um fourth
quattuor, *indecl. adj.* four
-que, *conj.* and
queō, quīre, quiī/quīvī to be able
quī, quae, quod who, which, that
quīcumque, quaecumque, quodcumque, *indef. rel. prn.* anyone/anything whatever
quid, *adv.* why?
quīdam, quaedam, quoddam, *indef. prn.* a certain; *pl.* some
quidem, *adv.* indeed
quiēs, quiētis, *f.* rest, repose
   sē quiētī dare, to rest (*lit.,* give oneself to rest)
quīndecim, *indecl. adj.* fifteen
quīntus, -a, -um fifth
quis, quid, *interrog. prn.* who?, what?
   following **sī, num, nisi, nē,** anyone
quisnam, quidnam who/what, tell me?
quisquam, quicquam, *indef. prn.* anyone/anything at all
quisque, quaeque, quidque, *distrib. prn.* each one
quō, *interrog.* (to) where?
quod, *conj.* because
quoque, *adv.* also

– R –

rāmus, -ī, *m.* branch of a tree
rāna, -ae, *f.* frog
recipiō, recipere, recēpī, receptus to take back

recumbō, recumbere, recubuī to recline, lie down
reddō, reddere, reddidī, redditus to give back, return
redeō, redīre, rediī to go back, return
redimō, redimere, redēmī, redēmptus to buy back; to ransom
rēgia, -ae, *f.* royal palace
rēgīna, -ae, *f.* queen
rēgius, -a, -um royal
regnum, -ī, *n.* kingdom
regō, regere, rexī, rectus to govern, rule
regredior, regredī, regressus sum to return, go back
rēgulus, -ī, *m.* petty king; king's son
relinquō, relinquere, relīquī, relictus to leave behind
rēs, reī, *f.* thing, matter, business, situation
   rēs domestica the housework
   rē vērā, *adv.* really, for sure
remōtus, -a, -um far removed, far away
respondeō, respondēre, respondī to reply, answer
retineō, retinēre, retinuī, retentus to hold onto, detain, restrain
reveniō, revenīre, revēnī to come back to, return
revertō, revertere, revertī to return, revert
rēx, rēgis, *m.* king
rīdiculus, -a, -um laughable
rīpa, -ae, *f.* bank (of a river)
rīsus, -ūs, *m.* laugh

rīvus, -ī, *m.* stream
rōdō, rōdere, rōsī, rōsus to gnaw, nibble, bite
rogō, rogāre, rogāvī, rogātus to ask
Rōma, -ae, *f.* Rome
Rostra, -ōrum, *n. pl.* speaker's platform (in the Forum at Rome)
rostrum, -ī, *n.* muzzle (of animal), beak (of bird)
ruber, rubra, rubrum red
rūfus, -a, -um red
rūrsus, *adv.* again
rūs, rūris, *n.* the countryside; a country estate
  rūrī (*locative*) in the countryside
rūsticus, -ī, *m.* peasant, country person

– S –

saevus, -a, -um savage, fierce
sagācitās, sagācitātis, *f.* wisdom, insight
saliō, salīre, saliī, saltus to jump
Saliāris, -e belonging to the **Saliī,** the priests of Mars who were famous for sumptuous banquets
Saliī, -ōrum, *m. pl.* priests of Mars who performed ritual dances (and held banquets)
saltō, saltāre, saltāvī to dance
saltātrīx, saltātrīcis, *f.* dancing girl
salūs, salūtis, *f.* safety
salūtō, salūtāre, salūtāvī, salūtātus to greet
salvē, salvēte greetings!, hello!
salvus, -a, -um safe
sanguineus, -a, -um blood-red
sapiō, sapere, sapīvī to be tasty, to taste good

scālae, -ārum, *f. pl.* a ladder
scelerōsus, -a, -um wicked, evil
sciō, scīre, scīvī, scītus to know
sē, *3rd pers. refl. prn. (acc./abl.)* himself, herself, itself, oneself; themselves
secundus, -a, -um the next, the following, the second
sed, *conj.* but
sedeō, sedēre, sēdī to sit
seges, segetis, *f.* crop (of corn or other grain)
sella, -ae, *f.* chair
semper, *adv.* always
senex, senis, *m.* old man
septem, *indecl. adj.* seven
sequor, sequī, secūtus sum to follow
serō, serere, sēvī, satus to sow (seeds)
servō, servāre, servāvī, servātus to save, preserve
serviō, servīre, servīvī to serve, be a slave to
sex, *indecl. adj.* six
sī, *conj.* if
sibi, *3rd pers. reflex. prn. (dat.)* to/for himself, herself, itself, oneself; themselves
sīc, *adv.* thus(ly), in this way
silva, -ae, *f.* forest, woods
silvestris, -e of the forest, in the woods
simul, *adv.* together, at the same time
simul atque, *conj.* as soon as
sinus, -ūs, *m.* fold (of one's garment); breast, lap
sistō, sistere, stetī, status halt, come to a stop

situs, -a, -um placed, located
solea, -ae, *f.* sandal
sōlus, -a, -um alone
sollemne, -is, *n.* a religious ceremony
sollicitus, -a, -um anxious, worried
solum, -ī, *n.* the ground
solvō, solvere, solvī, solūtus to pay, give in payment
somnus, -ī, *m.* sleep
spatium, -ī, *n.* space
speciēs, speciēī, *f.* appearance
spectō, spectāre, spectāvī, spectātus to look at, watch, observe
speculum, -ī, *n.* mirror
splendidus, -a, -um bright, shining, dazzling
sportella, -ae, *f.* a small basket
squāleō, squālēre, squāluī to be unkempt, lie waste
statim, *adv.* immediately
sternūtō, sternūtāre, sternūtāvī to sneeze repeatedly or violently
stō, stāre, stetī to stand
stola, -ae, *f.* woman's long dress
strāmenta, -ōrum, *n. pl.* straw (used as material for animal bedding, etc.)
strepitus, -ūs, *m.* noise, racket, clattering
structor, structōris, *m.* builder, mason
stultus, -a, -um foolish, stupid, slow-witted
suāvis, -e sweet
suāviter, *adv.* sweetly
sub, + *abl.* (*of location*), + *acc.* (*of motion*), under

subitō, *adv.* suddenly
sum, esse, fuī to be
sumptuōsus, -a, -um expensive, costly, extravagant
surgō, surgere, surrēxī to rise, get up
sustineō, sustinēre, sustinuī to support, withstand, endure

– T –

tablīnum, -ī, *n.* study, office
taenia, -ae, *f.* ribbon
taeter, taetra, taetrum foul, vile, monstrous
tam, *adv.* so, to such an extent
tamen, *adv.* however, nevertheless
tandem, *adv.* finally, at last
tantus, -a, -um so great, so much
  tantī of so much worth (*gen. of value*)
  tantō (by) so much (*abl. degree of difference*)
tē, *2nd pers. sing. prn.* (*abl. and acc.; nom.* **tū**) you
tēctum, -ī, *n.* roof
temptō, temptāre, temptāvī, temptātus to attempt, try
tempus, temporis, *n.* time
tenuis, -e thin, weak
tergum, -ī, *n.* back
tertius, -a, -um third
theātrum, -ī, *n.* theater
tibi, *2nd pers. sing. prn.* (*dat.; nom.* **tū**) to/for you
timidus, -a, -um fearful
tin, (onomatopoeia; sound of a bell ringing)
tintinnābulum, -ī, *n.* bell

tintinnō, tintinnāre to make a ringing sound
tortus, -a, -um (*participle of* **torquēre**) twisted, bent
tōtus, -a, -um the whole
trādō, trādere, trādidī, trāditus to hand over
trahō, trahere, traxī, tractus to pull, draw, drag
   lānam trahere to spin wool
trāns, + *acc.*, across
trānseō, trānsīre, trānsiī to go across
trānsferō, trānsferre, trānstulī, trānslātus to carry across
trēs, tria three
trīstis, -e sad, mournful
trīticum, -ī, *n.* wheat crop
trux, trucis rough, forbidding, harsh
tū, *2nd pers. sing. prn. (nom.)* you
tum, *adv.* then
turpis, -e shameful, base, disgusting
   turpissimum, -ī, *n.* most shameful thing (a most unkind way to address a person)
tuus, -a, -um your, belonging to you (*sing.*)
tuxtax, (onomatopoeia; a thumping sound, used of falling blows on a person, in Plautus)

– U –

ubi, *interrog.* where?
ubīque, *adv.* everywhere
ūllus, -a, -um any
ulterior, ulterius further, more distant
umquam, *adv.* ever
ūnā, *adv.* together
ūnus, -a, -um one, the only
ursa, -ae, *f.* she-bear
ursulus, -ī, *m.* bear cub (*dimin. of* **ursus**)
ursus, -ī, *m.* bear
usque, *adv.* all the time, all the way, right until
ut, *conj.* so that, in order that, with the result that (+ *subjunctive*); as (+ *indicative*)
ūtor, ūtī, ūsus sum to use (+ *abl.*)
ūvae, -ārum, *f. pl.* grapes
uxor, uxōris, *f.* wife

– V –

vacca, -ae, *f.* cow
vādo, vādere to go, advance, proceed
valdē, *adv.* very
valē, valēte farewell!
valeō, valēre, valuī to be well, have (enough) strength
valētūdō, valētūdinis, *f.* health, condition of body
vehiculum, -ī, *n.* vehicle, conveyance
vendō, vendere, vendidī, venditus to sell
venēnum, -ī, *n.* poison
veniō, venīre, vēnī to come
venustās, venustātis, *f.* charm, grace, beauty
vepres, veprium, *f. pl.* thornbushes
verrō, verrere to sweep
versicolor, versicolōris parti-colored; of different colors, variegated

vertō, vertere, vertī, versus to turn, change (something) into
  sē vertere to change into
vērus, -a, -um true
  ita vērō, *adv.* yes, yes indeed
  rē vērā, *adv.* really, for sure
vesper, *m.* (*gen. not attested*) evening
vester, vestra, vestrum belonging to you (*pl.*)
vestīmentum, -ī, *n.* clothing
vestītus, -ūs, *m.* clothing, suit of clothing
via, -ae, *f.* road, route, way
vicissim, *adv.* in turn, in alternation
victus, -ūs, *m.* way of life, livelihood
videō, vidēre, vīdī, vīsus to see
videor, vidērī, vīsus sum to seem, appear
vīlla, -ae, *f.* country house
vīnea, -ae, *f.* vineyard
vir, virī, *m.* man, husband
  vir optime (*voc.*) sir

viridis, -e green
vīsitō, vīsitāre, vīsitāvī, vīsitātus to visit
vīta, -ae, *f.* life
  vītam agere to lead a life
vitreus, -a, -um made of glass
vīvō, vīvere, vīxī to live
vōbīs, 2nd pers. pl. prn. (*dat./abl.; nom.* **vōs**) for you, with you
vocō, vocāre, vocāvī, vocātus to call, summon
volō, volāre, volāvī to fly
volō, velle, voluī to want
vorō, vorāre, vorāvī, vorātus to devour
vōs, 2nd pers. pl. prn. (*nom./acc.*) you
vōx, vōcis, *f.* voice
vulnerō, vulnerāre, vulnerāvī to injure, wound
vulpēs, vulpis, *f.* fox
vultus, -ūs, *m.* face, appearance, countenance

Student-Friendly Readers

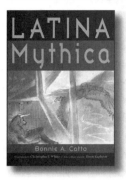

Latina Mythica

Bonnie A. Catto
Illustrations by Christopher J. White

xiv + 202 pp. (2006) 6" x 9" Paperback, ISBN 978-0-86516-599-1

This intermediate Latin reader with high-interest stories from Greek and Roman mythology boosts reading speed and reader confidence. The level of difficulty is graduated, with earlier stories being easier than those that come later. All stories are patterned after ancient authors: a perfect way to ease into advanced and author reading courses.

Each story includes an introduction in English and citation for the ancient sources of the myths. Stories are also accompanied by discussion questions and overviews of the cultural influences of each myth in art, music, ballet, and literature.

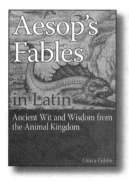

Aesop's Fables in Latin

Laura Gibbs

xxv + 356 pp. (2009) 7" x 10" Paperback, ISBN 978-0-86516-695-0

Aesop's Fables in Latin allows students to review grammar and syntax and increase their knowledge of Latin prose style while they read eighty Aesop's fables in Latin prose, taken from the seventeenth-century edition illustrated by Francis Barlow. These Latin prose fables are simple, short, witty, and to-the-point, with a memorable moral lesson. Forty original black-and-white Barlow illustrations and 129 pertinent Latin proverbs appear throughout the text. Selected fables include many that have become proverbial, such as "The Tortoise and The Hare" and "The Dog in the Manger," along with lesser known fables.

This is the perfect ancillary for intermediate students, to increase comprehension, confidence, and enthusiasm for reading Latin.